Bre...
so great
meet you!

THE
DARK ONES

by
Rachel Van Dyken

The Dark Ones
by Rachel Van Dyken

THE DARK ONES
Copyright © 2015 RACHEL VAN DYKEN
ISBN 13: 978-1515246701
ISBN: 1515246701
Cover Art Designed by P.S. Cover Design

*To my AMAZING fan group Rachel's New Rocking Readers!
I LOVE having you guys do group beta reads of my books.
Thanks for helping me out with this one
and being a part of the creative process; you are amazing!*

CHAPTER ONE

Genesis

I WAS NEVER ONE TO BE accused of being patient. Then again, I'd never understood the need for patience. To me, patience meant that I was either in the process of getting lectured or about to get lectured. I chewed the edge of my thumbnail and waited in the darkness.

"Ugly." My mother shook her head in my direction. "Remember that... you will always be ugly to them."

Them.

The very word dripped with hatred. You'd think after centuries of working together, we'd have found a happy medium. My mother had her own reasons for hating them, and up until this point, I'd had exactly none.

I'd spent my entire existence balancing my normal school life with my folklore studies, something I'd always hated but it had been necessary, just in case my number was called.

My entire family had a bad reputation for going against the rules, against the calling that had been given them, so I'd never been really concerned about being called in.

Until now.

I'd been eating soggy cereal, staring into the Corn Chex, when my mother's scream erupted through the house, followed by her passing out and my dad needing to call the paramedics.

Her heart had stopped. Literally. Stopped.

All because of a phone call.

Naturally, my parents had lied and said she'd been having chest pain, but I knew the truth.

It was fear.

Fear had stopped her heart, almost resulting in her death.

And fear was about to stop mine.

"Stop," Mother hissed at my side. "Do you want them to think you're a barbarian?"

To them? I already was, so I didn't really see the point in pretending to be anything else. To those individuals, I would always be the dirt beneath their feet, the little plaything they had to put up with.

I knew their history.

Probably better than most of them.

I'd been studying them for most my life, pouring over books and research with constant dread that, one day, my number would be called, and my life would be played out for me in absolute horror.

Humans were like little insects that they allowed to survive only because it was necessary for their own survival. We die. They die. Therefore, we live.

The darkness lifted for a few brief minutes as the door creaked open.

"Genesis?" a seductive male voice spoke into the darkness. "They will see you now."

My mom, with her long dark hair and bright green eyes, gave me one more look and shook her head. "Remember, you are nothing, you are ugly, you are humble, you are stupid, you aren't brave, you are nothing. You. Are. Nothing."

I nodded and repeated the mantra in my head.

The same one she'd pounded into my skull since my birth. She'd had her reasons, not that it made hearing those words any easier. Several times during my upbringing, I'd locked myself in my room and just stared at myself in the mirror. I'd focused on each feature and wondered what was so horrible about my eyes, my lips, my face — even my cheeks — that I had to repeat those ugly words until I was blue in the face.

The one time I'd asked her, she'd snorted and said something about our bloodlines being wicked and selfish, and how the females in our family were not known for our humility.

Basically, my own mother believed that if my number was called...

I would be killed.

My sarcastic nature didn't help things, and if my number was called, I figured it would get my tongue cut out.

And even though it was 2015, and I thought we'd come a long way with equality and human rights...

I was still nothing. In their eyes I was both nothing and everything, all wrapped up into one.

Human.

Special.

But unable to grasp my own uniqueness because of my imperfect creation.

"Nothing," I chanted under my breath. "I am nothing."

My black, over-the-knee boots clicked against the concrete as I made my way toward the light, the only light in the room, peeking out from the grand doorway.

I'd chosen to wear black leggings with a wraparound cream sweater, hoping that if I covered enough of myself, it would look humble, but not so humble that I didn't at least try to look nice for my meeting.

I'd never been the most secure girl in the world. Then again, how could I have confidence when every day of my life my mom had repeated that same mantra in my head? *"You are nothing."*

I sensed a sudden presence at my back. A hand, I realized. The contact made me gasp. A slight warm tingle ran through and somehow down my neck.

"Sorry," a man said to my right. I couldn't see him yet, but his voice sounded like a soothing melody, causing me to almost sway on my feet. "I forget how fragile humans can be."

I nodded. "It's okay."

"This way." The pressure from his hand wasn't necessarily painful, but it wasn't pleasant either, almost like an electric current was passing from his body into mine. I'd heard that it was nearly impossible to turn off certain powers — it would be like me trying to tell my heart to stop beating.

Once I was through the door, I looked around.

It was magnificent.

The floor was a dark black marble; the walls had sconces that I'm sure at one point had held torches — before electricity.

Two large doors stood in my way. I could feel the power on the other side; the room practically sang with it.

"Do not speak," the man on my right said. Finally, I glanced up and closed my mouth immediately.

What would a perfectly healthy twenty-five-year-old say to someone who had no eyes? Only dark spots where eyes once were?

Not to mention, his mouth wasn't moving, yet he was speaking.

I knew what he was.

"Fear isn't welcome here." He spoke again, this time rubbing my back as if to comfort me. But his mouth still didn't move. Regardless of the knowledge in my head about this type of creature, I was still having trouble breathing.

This was really happening.

My number had been called.

I was at the ceremony.

My life was going to change forever.

To run away would mean death.

To take a few more steps — well, it meant the same thing. Especially if I didn't please them.

I tugged at my sweater, my palms sweating.

"You look lovely, just remember. No fear. You are nothing. You are everything. You are simply... you." He nodded again and the two oak doors opened.

A gasp escaped between my lips before I could stop it.

"They have that effect on everything," he whispered.

And then the lights brightened.

All the schooling in the world couldn't have prepared me for what I saw. All the pictures, all the movies, all the preparation.

And suddenly, I wanted very much to fall to my knees and cry.

CHAPTER TWO

Genesis

"GO ON," THE MAN URGED.

I took another step forward.

And suddenly he was gone. The doors shut behind me. I was completely and utterly alone.

Facing *them*.

Was I allowed to look directly at them? Was I supposed to speak? I had no idea what the protocol was, only that if I broke it, I wouldn't even feel pain before they sliced me up and tossed my parts back to where I'd come from.

I held my head high and waited, all the while repeating the same mantra in my head. *"I'm nothing, I'm nothing. I'm everything."*

"Genesis." A smooth voice called my name. It was so beautiful on his lips I wanted to cry again, and I'd never thought myself an overly emotional person, one of the only things my mom had applauded me for.

Slowly, I turned to the left. A man dressed in dark jeans and a white T-shirt stood from a silver throne. His hair was impossibly light, almost white, his eyes a glowing blue.

He was smiling.

It looked painful on him.

Only because it was so beautiful.

"Fear isn't welcome here." He repeated the same thing the first man had said.

"Apologies... sir." Or was it my lord? I couldn't remember and hoped it wouldn't be the last thing I uttered. How bad would that suck? Not that I'd be alive to actually care.

"Ah..." A blindingly white smile flashed in my direction as heat from his body flew at me in waves, nearly sending me to my knees. From my fingers all the way down to my toes, I wanted to touch him. I wanted to taste him. It was more than just being near him — I wanted everything about him to consume me until I wasn't even me anymore.

Don't you though? His voice sounded in my mind.

I blinked, trying to stay strong as the pieces fell together. He was a male siren, someone so sensual, so strong in his sexuality that he couldn't help but give off pheromones by merely breathing. Our books hadn't mentioned male sirens, but I couldn't imagine him being anything but that. He was too perfect, too strong, too warm. My body hummed with awareness.

"Beautiful, isn't she?" he said, the waves getting hotter and hotter, making me want to whimper aloud. I wanted to touch him, any part of him, even his feet. How stupid was that? I would literally sell my soul if I could touch his big toe.

He threw his head back and laughed. "This should be fun."

"Alex, stop it," a woman said to his right. "She's shaking."

"So am I." He winked.

Something flew by his head, barely missing his chin.

"Damn it, Stephanie, let me have my fun."

"You have fun," the woman rolled her eyes, "every day. Now sit down before you give her a heart attack."

Alex sat, the waves slowly dissipated, and I was able to

focus on the woman next to him. They could have been twins, except she wasn't just beautiful, but absolutely flawless — her eyes were the same bright blue, and she was wearing one of the dresses I'd seen at Nordstrom the week before... the price tag had been too high, and I'd been convinced that even if I'd put it on, it would look dumpy on me.

Because my mother's voice chimed in my head, *"You are nothing."*

I clenched my fists tighter and managed a head nod in her direction.

When my eyes fell to the third person in the room, I took a step back.

"Fear is not welcome here," the man barked, his eyes black and cold.

"Right," I whispered. "I'm — I'm sorry."

His lips twitched. Where the others were bright and pretty, he had shaggy brown hair that hung past his shoulders and black eyes that seemed to see right through me; his smile was attractive but predatory, and I was pretty sure that if he wanted to break me in half just to prove he could, he'd only need to use two fingers.

"You're different from the others."

I wasn't sure if different was good or bad; it was on the tip of my tongue to ask, but I thought better of it when he leaned forward, causing my heartbeat to sky rocket.

He was a beast or werewolf. I'd studied his kind, even though it had terrified me to go over those chapters in class. They were unpredictable, angry, scary hunters that thought emotions were for the weak.

It was believed they lacked the ability to empathize with others, making them one of the most dangerous creatures to humans.

He was proving the text hadn't lied. No smile. No light behind his eyes, just emptiness.

"You really are a pretty one, aren't you?" another voice

chimed in, this one deep, smooth, soothing… like a stream where the water trickled over the rocks.

Giving my head a shake, I turned to the man next to the werewolf and barely managed to hold in a gasp.

He was gorgeous.

Light green eyes glowed in my direction, beamed and twinkled with each blink, almost like I was staring at stars. His skin was smooth and light. Dark brown hair was pulled back into a low ponytail, and he had a leather bomber jacket on.

He was the epitome of every girl's fantasy come to life.

I quickly averted my eyes, aware I was blatantly staring at him.

"What?" His warm chuckle made my body tingle. "Are you afraid to look at me, human?"

"No." I found my voice, "Not at all." Slowly I lifted my gaze to his and waited.

His smile was blinding. "Good, that's good, as we'll be spending many hours together in the near future." His smile suddenly dropped as if the idea saddened him, or maybe just made him want to kill me and get it over with.

Yeah, that was what I was afraid of.

Maybe I was better off with the werewolf.

Or the siren.

"Enough." A booming voice sounded throughout the room, shaking me out of my stare-down with the man. Only vampires had green eyes, so I imagined that was what he was, though he looked nothing like I imagined a vampire would look.

I glanced around for the location of the voice but saw nothing.

The smile froze on the vampire's face. He shared a look with the others and leaned back in his chair, while the other three seemed to stiffen in theirs, as if they were afraid. What could they possibly have to fear? They were immortal.

I looked around the room again. The lights flickered.

That couldn't be a good sign.

Up until now, I'd had no idea what immortals I'd be meeting with, and I wracked my brain trying to think of who else would be there — who else I should be afraid of... when suddenly the room went black.

It was only three seconds.

But it was enough for my brain and survival instincts to kick in.

I had to force my feet to stay planted.

I had to force the scream to stay in my throat.

And when I felt a hand reach out and touch my shoulder, the pain I felt at that touch was so life-altering that I fell to my knees, my body giving out.

"That's better," the voice said. "Don't you know you are to kneel in front of those you serve?"

"S-sorry," I said through clenched teeth. "It won't happen again."

"No," he said, "it won't. Because if it does, you'll be dead. Understand?"

"Yes."

The ice from his touch wouldn't let up; it continued to flow through my body like he was trying to freeze every vein I had.

The lights flickered again, and then he was standing in front of me.

All seven feet of him.

It hurt to stare.

But not as much as it would have if I hadn't — I, at least, had paid attention to that part of my studies. To look away was like experiencing the greatest pain imaginable because, as a human, I was drawn to his beauty, drawn to his essence in a way that had been programmed since the beginning of time.

He was a Dark One.

A fallen.

Half angel. Half human.

And he was the leader of the immortals. His punishment, along with the others of his kind had been to watch over both races, keeping them as separate as possible while still making sure both thrived. Requiring him to live with humans and play police with the immortals was a punishment.

They were called Dark Ones because both light and dark fought for them, making it impossible for lights to stay on or the dark to stay dark for too long a time span.

They commanded the dark.

But were forced to live in the light.

They were equal parts good and bad, which made them the most dangerous as they had no moral compass.

"Interesting..." His head tilted in a cat-like stance. "...that you know so much about me. Pray tell, are you going to give us a history lesson? You may stand."

Crap. I stood on shaky feet.

They could also read thoughts if they wanted to.

Though most weren't powerful enough to do so.

"I am."

Those two words devastated me. If he was that powerful, he wasn't just any Dark One. He was—

"Cassius." He finished my thought, his lips tilting up in a seductive smile. White teeth flashed, and then he turned on his heel, slowly walking up the stairs to where everyone else was seated. "But to you..." He turned slightly, his eyes flashing white before going back to a normal blue. "...I am Master."

CHAPTER THREE

Genesis

CASSIUS. THE NAME BURNED ON MY lips though I hadn't spoken it out loud — was too afraid to. I knew the power behind his name, behind who he was.

He was like a god to the immortals.

And to me?

Well, he was more than that. He could kill me with a simple snap of his fingers. He could make me see my worst nightmares by simply willing it to happen. But worst of all? He could own me. It was said that Dark Ones treated humans as pets, playthings — an amusement. But because Dark Ones had such heightened emotions, when they abandoned a human out of boredom or something else trivial, it killed the human.

Instantly shattering their hearts in their chests.

Once the Dark Ones were finished with you — you didn't survive it. No one could survive the emotional break that came when someone like Cassius left.

It was emptiness.

It was death.

I needed to stay far, far away from him if I wanted to live.

The only happy thought that occurred to me was that someone as old as Cassius most likely despised humans enough not to toy with them. Unlike the vampire and siren, who found it amusing and harmless.

"Do you know your duties?" Cassius barked. "Or am I to go over them with you? From the looks of Alex, it seems he's been too preoccupied to do much of anything except fill the air with his arousal."

Alex's nostrils flared, but he said nothing.

"And, Stephanie, what's your excuse?"

She dropped her head and gave a little shudder. "Sorry, Cassius."

"Mason?" He turned to the werewolf. "Your looks don't betray you, but your rapid heartbeat does. Tell me, does she set your blood on fire?"

The werewolf rolled his eyes. "Only in irritation, my lord."

"Ethan..." Cassius barked. "You've been quiet."

"I've been watching." Ethan tilted his head, making himself look more vampire than before. The way his eyes glowed in my direction sent shivers all the way down my spine. "I think I'll keep her."

Stephanie jumped up from her seat. "Ethan—!"

"Please." Ethan waved her off. "He owes me, don't you, Cassius?"

The temperature in the room dropped at least thirty degrees while Cassius stood and, with little effort, threw Ethan across the room. He slammed into one of the rock walls.

Pieces of dust flew into the air. I gasped, covering my mouth with my hands.

"Dramatic," Ethan huffed beneath an array of rubble and rock. "Then again, you've always been dramatic, haven't you, Dark One?"

Cassius released Ethan and turned to face me. "You will go with Ethan. You will do your... duty." The way he said it made me feel dirty, like I was being whored out.

"I don't need to explain the rules, but I will, for your sake, explain them once. You're hired to do a specific job for us. You are not here to try to land yourself an immortal husband, so leave those hopes and dreams at the door. Physical contact between you and an immortal is forbidden, and if you are on the receiving end of it, outside of your duties, *you* will be the one punished, not the immortal."

Yeah, that was what I was afraid of.

"They may touch you, may do whatever the hell they want with you. But if you seek them out, touch them without proper invitation…" His voice trailed off, his nostrils flared. "Do you understand?"

Not at all. But I had no choice. I gave a quick nod, wringing my hands together. "Yes."

"Ethan," Cassius turned, "consider my debt paid."

Ethan's smile grew to gigantic proportions. "Oh, it's been paid," he licked his lips, "in full."

I knew that look.

I was going to die.

Because there was no way that vampire wasn't putting his hands or his fangs on me — and it would be my fault because I was the human.

To them, we weren't victims. Just nuisances they put up with.

"Well then…" Ethan held out his hand in my direction. "Shall we?"

Fear kept me rooted to my spot.

Then suddenly warmth spread throughout the room. I quickly glanced to the siren; Alex had his hand raised in the air, and I could almost see the heat radiating from his hand toward my body.

Be calm, he whispered in my head. *Ethan will not harm you.*

And you?

None of us mean you harm.

My gaze flickered to Cassius.

Alex gave a slight shake of his head. *Yes, human. He means you harm. You are never to be alone with him. Ever. If you are, I cannot help you. I cannot shield you from his power. If he touches you, if he claims you, it will be the last time you own your own body, soul, and mind. He will destroy you. If you must... run.*

My hands shook at my sides, but I managed a nod in his direction.

Ethan held out his hand again. "Come."

I followed him, careful not to touch his hand lest he have the same effect on me a Dark One would, and followed him through a side door.

He moved silently next to me, opening door after door, finally leading me into a dark parking garage where a black unmarked town car was waiting.

"Hurry, get in."

"What?"

He shoved me in the car and ran to the other side, faster than my eyes could follow, then sped off as if we were being chased.

"We don't have much time." He looked behind him. "Damn it, we have less than that much time."

"What are you talking about?"

"He will *hunt* you."

"What?" I gasped. "Who?"

"Cassius..." He spat. "He wants you. I could feel it. Could see it in his mind's eye as if I was living it myself. The reason you're here isn't for the immortals. It's for him."

"But, my mom said that—"

Ethan barked out a laugh. "Yes please tell me what your human mother told you about what your job is to the immortals?"

I swallowed the dryness in my throat. "I'm to educate you about the ways of the humans so you don't have to interact with us. Teach any of the immortal children how to use the

Internet, cell phones — technology — and at the end of the day, I—"

He roared with laughter, interrupting what I thought was a pretty good speech.

"So that's what they tell you now?"

"Wh-what?" I looked behind me only because he kept looking behind us. For Cassius to fly overhead? Or what? We were in the middle of Seattle. It's not like the immortal would want to be seen.

"Immortals cannot have children with one another, Genesis."

"What?" I gasped. "But that's impossible. That would mean—"

Ethan's eyes flashed. "Do you really think that with all the money we have, all the resources, we would need a tiny pitiful ugly little human to tell us how to use a damn computer?"

Well, when he put it that way…

It didn't make sense. I mean, I'd studied their history, studied everything about each race. I'd studied my butt off so I could be useful for them, to them. And when all of that was finished, I'd even had to take classes on proper etiquette — how to serve at an immortal feast, how to dress when I was presented, how to—

"Oh, my gosh," I gasped, reaching for the seatbelt.

Ethan's hands went to mine. "Stop. It will pass. You're just scared."

"But—"

"Shhh." Something shifted in the car, maybe it was the temperature, maybe it was just Ethan trying to calm me down, but my heartbeat slowed way down.

"Did you just…" My words felt funny. "…slow down my heart?"

"I'm a vampire, love. What did you expect me to do? Bite you into silence?"

Yeah, that's exactly what I expected; it's what the books

had said.

"Don't believe everything you read. Besides, I'm not the least bit hungry." He winked and took the next exit toward Lake Washington.

"So..." He drove the car like a maniac. Turns weren't just turns. It was like he was jerking the car so hard the steering wheel was about to come off. "Tell me you believe me."

"Believe you?"

"About your purpose?"

"What is my purpose?" I asked. "I mean, sir, or... um..." Crap, I'd drawn a blank on how I was supposed to address him. He was above me; I needed to show him respect.

"Ethan." He sighed heavily. "Damn, do they brainwash you that much these days?"

"These days?"

"We haven't called a number up in fifty years." Ethan shook his head. "Pity that Cassius would do it now. Then again, after looking at you..." He licked his lips. "...I'd probably do the same damn thing."

"What?"

"Home!" Ethan screeched the car to a halt in front of a gigantic, fenced-in mansion overlooking the lake. A few men stood outside the gates. When they magically swung open, Ethan sped inside then turned off the car. "Come on."

With no other option but to follow, I quickly got out of the car and followed him to the door.

Two men with the same-colored eyes but darker hair glanced from me to Ethan and back again.

The first spoke. "Apologies, my lord, but she... you cannot bring a breeder into the house! Not if you want to live through the night." He leaned forward and sniffed. "She's marked!"

"Stay out of it, Ben." Ethan gripped my hand and jerked me into the house.

"Breeder?" I repeated. "What did he mean by that?"

"Silence, human." Ethan continued pulling me through

the house until finally stopping in a gourmet kitchen. "I don't know what to do with you yet. I don't suppose you'll take kindly to the doghouse out back or the nice water bowl with the name *Scratch* on it?"

My mouth dropped open. "A dog? You're going to treat me like your dog?"

"Joke." He smirked. "But good to know you're opposed to sleeping outside."

My knees threatened to give out. He must have noticed; in an instant I was in his arms being carried to the nearest chair.

"Humans," he whispered into my hair. "So fragile."

It didn't register I was in a vampire's arms. In fact, nothing was registering. Nothing was making sense, and I wasn't sure if I was even allowed to ask questions. It wasn't my place. My mom had made that clear.

I was terrified of doing the wrong thing — and suffering for it.

The room felt warm again. Warm and familiar. I looked up just as Stephanie and Alex rushed in the room.

"Your scent is all over the thing." Alex shook his head. "It's not enough."

Ethan hissed. "I've had her for fifteen minutes. He freaking marked her. What do you expect me to do?"

"Try harder," Alex clipped then turned his cold blue eyes toward me. "Sorry, little one, but this day's going to get a hell of a lot worse before it gets better."

"I'll do it," a third gruff voice said.

"Mason..." Ethan nodded. "...do your worst."

Mason grunted then held out his hand to me.

I didn't take it.

"Hell, Ethan, what did you do to her?" Mason rolled his eyes. "She's petrified."

"She's human," Stephanie pointed out.

"S-sorry." I shook my head. "I'm sorry that I'm scared."

They all stopped glaring at one another and instead

turned their full focus on me.

"Fear attracts immortals," Mason said plainly. "It would be good of you to stop shaking."

"Slow her heart." Stephanie slapped Ethan in the chest. "Hurry."

Rolling his eyes, Ethan focused in on me, and slowly my racing heart went back to normal.

"Mason," Alex barked, "hurry."

"Right." Mason took a step forward. "*We* won't hurt you... but it will hurt."

"What?"

"Just..." Ethan cursed and looked away. "...stay as still as possible, human."

"She has a name," Alex grumbled, earning a fiery look from both Ethan and Mason.

My breath hitched when Mason leaned down, gripping my shoulders, and softly nibbled on my neck. It felt good — until a slicing pain followed the nibbling.

I shrieked.

He didn't let go.

When I was about ready to pass out, he pulled back, his eyes completely black. "It didn't work."

"Shit." Ethan ran his hands through his hair.

"You have to do something." Stephanie looked toward Ethan. "He'll find her if you don't."

"What the hell do you expect me to do?" Ethan roared. "Bite her?"

The room fell silent. Didn't vampires bite?

Isn't that what the text had said?

Alex exhaled loudly. "I'll try, just don't get all pissed off when she melts into a puddle on the floor."

"Oh please." Stephanie rolled her eyes.

"Focus." Alex snapped his fingers in front of my face. "Let me try to at least smother his scent with mine."

His lips descended.

And I was being kissed — by a siren. Something the texts described as indescribable ecstasy.

I was too afraid to feel anything except for heat and desire.

My heartbeat picked up again. My body went damp and hot as his mouth moved against mine.

When he pulled back, it wasn't with a satisfied smirk but one of hopelessness. "I'm so sorry, little human."

"He'll come for her," Stephanie whispered, her eyes flickering to Ethan. "If he takes her—"

"I know," Ethan barked. "Don't you think I'm well aware of our own prophesy?"

"Yet we play right into it... every century," Alex muttered. "I thought... for a second, I thought this one would be different. It felt different, right?"

The room fell silent again.

"What..." My voice was hoarse. "...what am I really doing with you? Why was my number called?"

"Oh dear..." Stephanie plopped down into a seat. "Ethan didn't explain that?"

"Again, fifteen minutes," Ethan muttered under his breath. "And she's human. It's not like her capacity for learning new information has evolved."

I glared at him.

Mason chuckled.

"Honey..." Stephanie reached her hand across the table and placed it on mine. "Whatever your family has taught you is a lie. You aren't here to teach us or do anything of the sort. You're... you're a breeder."

"A breeder," I repeated. "Like a horse?"

Mason laughed harder. Well, at least I knew werewolves weren't out to kill me.

Ethan swore and sat down on the other side of me.

"We call numbers every fifty years to breed. Immortals cannot procreate with other immortals," he explained. "Humans are chosen based on their scent, strength..." He coughed and looked away. "Physical appeal."

"But I'm ugly," I blurted. "To you I'm ugly. We're ugly, we're nothing, we're—"

Ethan shook his head slowly. "And that's the greatest deception of all." His hands moved to my chin. "To us you're not ugly. You are absolute perfection."

"To a Dark One," Mason continued, "you're life itself."

CHAPTER FOUR

Genesis

MY BREATH HITCHED IN MY CHEST as I stared at the strangers around me. What did that even mean? Life itself? I was nothing. Why would I be taught humility and self-hate my whole life only to be told by the very ones I was supposed to fear that I was life itself?

"Jealousy," Ethan said softly, "quickly turns to envy. Envy is a dangerous thing because you end up wanting so desperately what you'd never been given in the first place. The greatest sin an immortal can commit is to laugh in the face of what we are… and want." His eyes were sad. "He wants you."

"To kill me?" I whispered hoarsely.

"No." Ethan cupped my chin with his smooth fingers. "He wants to possess you, and believe me when I say you'll like every part of that possession — until he leaves you. Dark Ones always leave, and you'll die."

"Maybe she's different," Stephanie said in a quiet voice.

"You'd be willing to sacrifice another?" Mason roared, slamming his fists onto the table. It split down the middle right in front of me.

Gasping, I slid my chair back and nearly fell out of it.

"How many times have we said we'd stop testing the prophecy?"

Stephanie looked down at her hands. "It's the only hope we have."

"Hope," Alex muttered. "What a sad, pathetic little word."

"We aren't letting Cassius have her." Ethan's green eyes flashed as he released my chin. "We won't repeat what happened last time."

"What happened last time?" I asked, knowing I'd probably regret the answer.

Mason's entire face crumpled with pain as he let out a howl and ran out of the room.

"Shit." Alex stared after him. "It's going to take hours to get him to come out of his state now."

"I'm so sorry." I held up my hands. "I had no idea—"

"Of course you don't," Ethan snapped. "You know nothing."

I am nothing.

I hung my head.

"Be easy on her," Stephanie said in a calm voice. "She's been brainwashed for quite awhile."

"Will he be okay?" I asked in a small voice. "The wer—" I was about to say *werewolf* and had to stop myself. "Mason? Will he be okay?"

"After he runs." Ethan hung his head. "Maybe if he eats something other than berries and the damn pinecones I keep finding in the upstairs bedroom."

Stephanie's lips pressed together in a small smile. "He finds comfort in the outside."

"Yeah, well, he's ruining my wood floors," Ethan grumbled.

"You live together?" I blurted.

All eyes fell to me. "All immortals live together in one sense or another." It was Ethan who kept answering my questions. "And you didn't offend Mason as much as remind him of what should have been... what could have been."

"Oh." I swallowed against the dryness in my throat. Shock must have been wearing off as I could at least feel my body again, though what I felt was shaky and weak.

"Ethan..." Stephanie glanced between us. "I know you don't like the idea, but it's really the only way."

He chewed his lower lip; fangs descended from the top of his mouth. "I know."

"It's the only thing we haven't tried." Alex put his arm around Stephanie. "It won't be so bad, will it?"

What were they talking about?

And why was I suddenly feeling rejected all over again?

"It won't be so bad," Ethan repeated. "It will be absolute torture... hell rising to earth... and you ask me to do this still? Knowing what you know?"

The two of them hung their heads but said nothing.

It was on the tip of my tongue to ask when the entire temperature in the room dropped.

I saw my own breath.

"He's close." Alex cursed. "Do it now!"

Ethan's green eyes met mine; they flashed then went completely black before he said in a low gravelly voice, "I'm so sorry."

All I felt was pain.

As black overtook everything.

"I LOVE YOU SO MUCH." The woman danced in the field, throwing her hands up into the air in excitement. "Say you love me."

"I love you." Ethan grinned. "Always, you know this."

"Say it again!" She laughed and threw herself into his arms.

I felt everything he felt, like it was me. He wasn't just elated, he was... perfect. Life was perfect. The universe was at one with him and his mate.

"The hour grows late," he whispered against her temple. "Shall we go back to the castle?"

She pulled away and pouted. Her dark hair fell in loose waves all the way down to her waist. "Catch me first."

"Too easy."

"Do it!" She laughed than took off ridiculously fast.

Laughing, Ethan chased her into the forest.

It was impossible not to laugh with them, not to experience the love firsthand. It was so beautiful I wanted to weep, but I couldn't feel my face or any part of my body. Maybe I was dead. But at least I'd seen true love once. It was something I'd never forget — the way he held her, the way their hearts beat the same rhythm.

The scene changed.

She was in a large bed. The curtains were pulled back from the window, letting in the moonlight.

"A son." She held the baby up in her arms and grinned. "Ethan, we have a son!"

Ethan's face was pure awe as he took the small bundle in his hands and whispered against the baby's head. "So perfect."

"He is."

"We did it," Ethan said with tears in his eyes. "I cannot believe after all these years—"

The temperature in the room dropped.

"Quickly..." Her eyes were fearful. "Take him away from here."

"He would never harm a child." Ethan shook his head. "We can trust him."

"We can't!" she cried. "You've seen what they are capable of."

"Leave it!" he roared. "I will protect us."

The door to the room burst open as Cassius casually walked in, his eyes scanning the room with a cold detachment that caused me to shiver.

"So..." Cassius tilted his head; it looked animalistic. "You defy me?"

"She's half human," Ethan said. "You know the rules."

"The rules..." Cassius grinned. "...and you've broken them."

"No." Ethan shook his head. "That's impossible."

The woman in the bed started to cry softly in her hands.

"Maybe you should ask your wife where her loyalty lies."

"Ethan..." she sobbed. "I'm so sorry! It was the only way! It was the only way!"

Realization dawned in Ethan's eyes as he fell to his knees. "Tell me you didn't do this, my love... tell me!"

No more words were spoken.

I felt like my heart was breaking right along with his.

Cold green eyes met mine as if he truly knew I was there, in that heaven or hell, in the dream.

"Awake!" he screamed.

I jolted up from the bed in a cold sweat. Ethan hovered over me, Stephanie rocked in the corner, and Alex paced the floor.

"It worked." Alex paused his walking, still not looking at me. "Thank God, it worked."

"Of course it did," Stephanie agreed; her eyes held such a deep sadness, my heart clenched in my chest. "Ethan..."

He shoved away from my bedside and walked out of the room, slamming the door behind him.

"He won't hurt you." Alex gave me a sympathetic smile. "Just... give him time."

"Time?"

Stephanie nodded. "To get used to the idea."

"The idea of what?"

"You're his new mate." Stephanie stood, just as the sound of a man screaming in agony pierced my ears. "We'll leave you now."

CHAPTER FIVE

Genesis

THE DOOR CLICKED SHUT, LEAVING ME completely and utterly alone. I pulled the blanket up to my chin and gave another jolt when another guttural roar came from somewhere in the house.

Ethan.

The minute I thought his name, I reached to my neck to see if he'd bitten me like Mason. Nothing but smooth skin met my fingertips, though my entire body still felt frozen — as if Cassius had marked me with a frigid temperature or something. But that was crazy.

In fact, the whole scenario was crazy.

I'd left every belonging I'd had with my mother, thinking I'd probably see her after I met with the immortals — she hadn't given me reason to believe otherwise.

I had no cell phone.

No money.

Absolutely no identification.

And, up until this point, I'd thought I'd been chosen to work for some secret society that hated me — but needed me desperately.

Instead, I'd been scared within an inch of my life.

And bitten twice — or at least I assumed twice.

My fingers grazed my neck again.

Nothing.

Another yell, this one hoarser than the ones before, as if Ethan was losing his voice.

I shivered and watched the flames flicker in the fireplace. The room they'd put me in was extravagant. I was lying in a king-sized bed with sheets that felt like silk against my fingers. A flat screen TV was positioned next to the fireplace, and pieces of artfully chosen furniture in tans and brown were scattered around, making everything look like I'd just stepped into Pottery Barn.

You know, if Pottery Barn included screaming as their background music.

Was I just supposed to wait until Ethan was done having a nervous breakdown? I mean, what was the protocol? My stomach growled on cue, reminding me that I hadn't eaten anything all morning.

Well, maybe if I starved to death, they wouldn't have to worry about me anymore. It seemed I was causing more trouble than anything.

My teeth chattered.

Why couldn't I get warm?

With a huff, I moved away from the bed and went to stand in front of the fireplace just as the door to my bedroom jerked open, nearly coming off the hinges.

Ethan stood in the doorway, blanketed in the warmth of the fire's glow. My breath hitched in my chest, even though I tried to stop my physical response. It was impossible — and embarrassing — knowing he probably heard my racing heart.

His hair was loose from the ponytail, falling around his sharp cheekbones and jaw.

His nostrils were flared as if he smelled something

horrific.

And when I opened my mouth to speak, he held up his hand and hissed at me.

Freaking hissed.

Like a cat.

I held my tongue and stared at the fire, thinking that was probably the best option for me at that point.

Get warm.

Funny, my entire life had been about rules, memorization, planning, and now I had one goal in life — to get warm and stay that way.

It was all I could allow myself to focus on. I was pretty sure if I let myself fully think about what had just happened to me, I'd have a nervous breakdown. After all, I was only human, something that was impossible to ignore with someone like Ethan standing next to me.

His fluid movement from the door to the fireplace was quick. I blinked, and he was standing next to me, holding his hands out.

I knew he could feel the heat, so I wasn't going to insult him by asking, even though it seemed like some of my studies had been clearly lacking. After all, I'd always thought vampires bit, but I had no bite marks, no recollection, nothing except blackness and the idea that his touch had been so painful I'd wanted to die.

"You are safe," he whispered in a hoarse voice. "Cassius won't be coming for you. He'd have to track you first."

"Am I untraceable now?" Now that I was his. Now that I didn't belong to myself anymore.

Ethan pulled his hand back from the air, clenching his fingertips into a tight fist. "To everyone but your mate."

"You." I closed my eyes and willed the tears to stay in. What was happening?

"Me," he confirmed.

My heart continued to race. I tried to glance at him out of

the corner of my eye, but when I did, those eyes — once green — were black and still trained on me. I didn't know vampires had black eyes, didn't know any part of their physiology — outside of their fangs — changed.

"The cold will pass," he said, still staring at me.

Finally, I turned to give him my full attention, hoping it wouldn't be the last thing I did. "Why am I so cold?" My teeth chattered as if to prove a point. I hugged my arms closer to my body and got closer to the fire.

"You'll be cold until he leaves you completely," Ethan said slowly. "I marked over him...took away what I could." His hand reached out cupping my face. "Soon you'll be warm again."

"B-because you're warm?"

He dropped his hand and smirked. "Scorching."

I was swaying toward him, not even realizing it, but his hands came out and steadied me then stayed. When he touched me, I could feel his heartbeat through his fingertips; it was addicting, fascinating. I moved closer. He didn't release me. His black eyes changed to more of a gray and then finally changed back to a flashing green as I moved into his arms. It was like I had no control over my body — I just wanted to be close.

And he was so warm.

And alive.

Very much alive.

His eyes hooded.

Inches apart — our lips were almost touching. My mind screamed at me to back away, but my body told me it was exactly where I needed to be.

"You're hungry." He twirled a piece of my hair with his fingertip then sniffed it. "I'll bring you food. Under no circumstances are you to leave this room until the marking is complete."

He released my hair. His other hand fell from my arm.

And the loss was heartbreaking.

"How will I know when it's complete?" I croaked out, like any terrified prisoner would.

His face cracked into a seductive smile before he looked away and his jaw clenched. "You'll know... because you'll be so on fire for me, you'll think of nothing else. Not food, water, safety — not anything. Your only need will be me."

I gulped. "Then what happens?"

He turned and walked to the door at a normal pace, pausing only to call over his shoulder, "I give you exactly what you need."

That's what I was afraid of.

CHAPTER SIX

Genesis

IT WAS AN HOUR LATER BEFORE any food was brought to me. I'd foolishly assumed it would be Ethan bringing food; instead, it was Alex.

I breathed a sigh of relief when he came into the room, tray of food in hand, and offered a shy smile — without the noticeable waves of seduction. Apparently, he could turn it off and on.

"Actually..." He sat the tray down on the bed and took a seat in the nearby chair. "...now that you're his mate, I could try my damnedest to seduce you, and you wouldn't feel a thing."

"Great," I croaked, reaching for a piece of toast.

"Mason cooked." Alex offered an apologetic yet radiant smile. "Word of warning, the man's been surviving on tree branches for the past twenty years, so if he's a little rusty in the kitchen, I apologize."

"Tree branches?" The toast was a bit dry, but it satisfied the hunger. I kept chewing, waiting for Alex to elaborate. Maybe he'd give me the answers I needed.

Alex propped his feet up on the bed. "His way of punishing himself, I suppose — ridiculous if you ask me. Then again, he's a werewolf, more beast than man. Who am I to judge?" His blue eyes twinkled briefly before he reached for the teakettle on my tray and poured some into one of the mugs. "Ethan didn't specify what to make for you. Sorry if we made a terrible mess out of things, but we mostly eat out every day, so there wasn't much food in the house — not to mention a vampire lives here so…"

I leaned forward, my eyes narrowing. "So he doesn't eat?"

Alex burst out laughing. "Just adorable. I may love you."

I scowled.

"Humans are funny," he said to himself more than to me. "I'd keep you if you weren't already being fought over and owned."

"I'm not a pet."

"Believe me when I say I treat my pets very well," he said in a low voice. "No complaints. Ever."

"Good for you." Arrogant much?

"Feeling the effects yet?" he asked, once I finished the toast and had moved on to the small slices of cheese and fruit. Crackers were on one side of the plate. Alex leaned forward, folding his massive hands in front of him. "A vampire's mark isn't something to be taken lightly."

"Well," I sighed, "I don't even know what the mark is, let alone what it should feel like. Apparently, I've been wrong about what I've been studying my entire life so, really, I don't know what to expect." I snorted. "You know, other than certain death if I disrespect any of you."

"That's still true," he said quickly. "With us four? Not so much. With the rest of them… keep your head down and try to say please and thank you."

"Noted."

"Fast learner."

"Survivor," I fired back.

He sighed, his smile slowly fading as did the light behind his blue eyes. "It's fifty-fifty."

"What?" I was just popping a piece of cheese into my mouth. Why did the food taste so bland? I was hungry — ravenous — so I didn't care, but it was like eating sandpaper.

"The survival rate, of course." Alex examined his fingernails then clicked his tongue. "Most humans are able to survive it, the strong ones."

"Survive what?" I clenched my teeth together as another chill wracked my body.

"The marking." His eyes narrowed. "It's made easier when your mate actually holds your damn hand through the process." I could have sworn he said ass under his breath, but it was too low to hear.

"He didn't..." I licked my lips and reached for a cracker. "He didn't want to do it though."

"Tough shit," Alex said in a louder voice, repositioning himself on the chair, dangling his legs off the side. "We've all had to make sacrifices for the greater good — this is his."

"Okay..." Feeling full and a bit sick, I put the cracker back on the plate. "And when this marking is all over... when I survive it — and believe me I will—"

Alex grinned, making me all the more irritated that he'd doubted my strength — that any of them would.

"What happens then? I'm Ethan's mate? I live to serve him, then I die? Only if Cassius doesn't ever find me?"

Alex went deathly still. "It's sad... tragic, actually... how little they tell you these days. About us. About the world and about your place in it."

"So tell me!" I pounded my fist into the pillow next to me, scaring the crap out of myself. I'd always been controlled — it had been bred into me from birth. And I'd just yelled at an immortal like he was a petulant child.

Alex grinned. "I think you'll do just fine, Genesis. Just fine." He chuckled warmly. "Try not to be too hard on us.

We've been waiting for a chance to change things for a very long time... and you just may be exactly what we've been waiting for."

"I can't do anything if you don't tell me what I'm supposed to be doing!" Tears threatened, the confusion and fear back full force. "I don't know what to do. Just tell me what I'm supposed to do."

"And that's the problem right there." Alex leaned forward, sadness etched in his every feature. "Your whole life, choices have been taken from you, rather than given to you." He hung his head. "I'll do this once and only once... I'll throw you a bone, isn't that what it's called? Do you a solid? A favor? And give you one goal this evening, one thing to set your small misinformed mind toward."

I waited in anticipation.

"Survive," he said softly. "Just survive. And when the flames threaten to take you higher and higher, give in. When the heat scorches you from the inside out, when tears no longer come, when the need is all you can contemplate... you survive."

He stood and shrugged, as if he hadn't just scared the crap out of me.

"Oh, and also? It would probably be good to call for your mate..." He offered a haphazard shrug. "When it's time."

"When I'm dying?"

"Only when your need is so great for him that you've forgotten yourself completely. That's when you whisper his name. Pray to God he answers — because he still has a choice in this, and if he doesn't choose you, survival will be pointless. You. Will. Die."

A lone tear fell down my cheek before I could wipe it away

Alex reached out and captured it with his thumb. "It's been years since I've seen real tears. I hope you keep yours. I hope the gift of feeling such strong emotions remains — then again — for your sake, at the same time, I hope they don't."

He left me.

Just like that.

With shaky hands, I put the tray on the nearby table and went back to lie on the bed, freaking out, wondering when the heat was going to come, when the pain would arrive, and when I would be out of my mind for a mate who clearly didn't want me.

A mate.

Like a husband.

Rejection washed over me.

I would never get *normal*.

Never have a family.

And most likely never have the type of love I'd always secretly wanted — it had all been stripped away from me the day I'd walked into that room. And a part of me hated my family for not telling me the truth about what I was about to do.

My mom had smiled.

And she'd probably known it was a death sentence.

I tried not to dwell on it — tried to stay positive — so I focused on what Alex said.

Survival.

I counted the seconds, the minutes as they turned into hours, and when the clock struck midnight out in the hall, I thought that maybe I would be different, maybe whatever was happening to me wasn't going to be as bad as both Alex and Ethan had warned.

Then the heat started in my toes.

I welcomed it because I'd been so cold all day.

It spread from my toes up my legs, warming me up like a blanket; by the time it reached my thighs, it was uncomfortable. I started throwing covers off me, but it didn't help.

Fire reached my chest, making it hard to breathe.

And when it touched my lips, it was like someone had placed coal in my mouth.

I cried out.

But no sound came.

I pounded my chest; the motion made the heat worse. I didn't think it could get more painful.

But it did. I glanced at the clock again.

It was two minutes past midnight.

And I already wanted to die.

The pain skyrocketed; I reared back, hitting my head on the headboard. Another surge of scorching heat flared.

The door opened, but my vision was blurred. It was hard to see who had come in.

It wasn't until he lay down on the bed next to me and grabbed my hand that I could focus on the form.

Mason.

As a werewolf.

Or a very large dog.

His eyes were sad.

And when I cried out again, he pulled me into his arms and squeezed while my body convulsed.

CHAPTER SEVEN

Genesis

HE WAS BEAUTIFUL. LONG BROWN HAIR cascaded past his shoulders — part of it was braided. Pieces fell by his perfectly sculpted face.

He smiled. His green eyes illuminated my whole world.

I reached for him, but each time my hands lifted, the burning was worse, so I learned to keep them behind me.

A sword was clasped in his right hand. He slid the blade across his left hand and held it in the air as blood dripped in slow motion onto the ground.

It was red until it touched the ground, turning into the same green I saw in his eyes. The green liquid seeped into the ground, nourishing it, causing grass and flowers to take root.

I gasped, reaching again.

The pain was too much.

He closed his eyes and cut again.

No! I tried yelling, but my voice simply didn't exist.

He continued, letting his blood spill around his feet. Hours went by, or maybe it was minutes. Soon an entire forest grew around us. I sighed in relief as the shield of the trees shaded me from the sun. The heat dissipated.

Only to return when Ethan looked at me again.

He turned and, in an instant, was in front of me, his black shirt open midway to his muscled chest.

We were in our own forest.

It started to rain.

I turned my face up, welcoming the cold.

But the raindrops weren't cold.

They were hot — searing hot.

The trees weren't protecting me anymore. I reached for Ethan, but he moved back. My need for shelter outweighed my need for him.

The scene changed. And suddenly I was standing near a river; he was on the other side.

I wanted him — I wanted the water more.

I tried jumping in, but each time I made a movement toward the water instead of him, the pain was unbearable.

With a silent sob, I fell to my knees.

When I looked up, Ethan was standing over me; he'd somehow made it past the river.

"When it's me you cry for — the pain ends."

I shook my head, fighting his words.

Because they meant the end of me. I knew it in my soul. If I gave in to the heat, if I gave into him, if I ignored my basic human needs — I wouldn't be human anymore.

I would be fully reliant on a strange being who didn't want me to begin with.

"Stop fighting it!" he roared.

I shook my head as heat consumed my body.

We were back in the throne room.

Cassius stood over me, his cold stare haunting. "And you still choose him? When I could give you relief?"

"Genesis, NO!" Ethan roared, but I couldn't see him.

All I could see, all I could feel was relief in Cassius's presence.

My body shook.

Cassius grinned, moving closer and closer to me.

The lesser of two evils.

Ethan.

I reared back; the heat got worse. I continued stepping backward until I was falling.

I landed in his arms.

His body was warm, not too hot, just warm enough to make me feel more comfortable.

"Genesis," Ethan whispered, his mouth near my ear. "Don't fight it."

"Don't..." I fought to get the words out. "Want. Me."

His eyes flashed green, and then his mouth was on mine.

It was like ice.

And all I saw was him.

All I wanted was him.

All I could think about was him.

As our heartbeats and breathing synced in perfect cadence with one another. I tugged his head harder toward mine — greedy for his lips, needing so desperately to taste him I thought I'd die.

With a cry I jolted awake from the dream.

To find myself not in Mason's arms — but Ethan's.

Completely.

Naked.

CHAPTER EIGHT

Genesis

I IMMEDIATELY TRIED TO RECOIL, ASHAMED, embarrassed, and horrified that I was in his arms without any clothes on. As if sensing my thoughts, Ethan looked away, jaw clenched. "You were taking them off."

"I was hot!" I yelled, happy that my voice was back but still shaking from the pain. It was still there — the searing heat — but it was bearable.

"I had it under control," a voice said from the corner.

I pulled the blankets and covered myself as Mason stepped out of the shadows, now looking like his normal self.

"You didn't need to interfere, Ethan."

"She's. Not. Yours." Ethan hissed.

"Now you claim me," I mumbled.

His jaw popped, as if he'd been trying to clench his teeth but had overdone it and nearly dislocated his entire face. "If you would have given in right away, your clothing wouldn't have been an issue!"

"So it's my fault." My lower lip trembled. "Is that what you're saying?"

"Damn it, Ethan." Mason made his way to the bed and threw another blanket over my body. I'd completely forgotten I was still naked — and arguing — probably because I was still so hot. "Just leave."

"She's my mate." Ethan released me but didn't leave his position next to me on the bed.

Mason hung his head. Dark circles framed his eyes. "Then do what's best for her. Just leave her be."

"If I leave, the marking won't be complete."

"She's been through enough this evening. Let her rest before the final stage. I think it's the least you can do... considering."

Ethan hung his head and whispered, "For my sacrifice... I'm the bad one in this scenario?"

"You became the bad one in this scenario the minute you heard your mate's screams and didn't come running. Now get out." Mason growled the last part so loud my ears started to ring.

Ethan cursed and stomped toward the door, leaving me.

I learned something in that instant.

He was a jerk.

No, he was a selfish ass.

But I missed him.

And I hated both him and myself because he'd turned away, and I needed him to be close.

My body yearned for him.

And the heat returned full force; I threw off the blanket then panicked and grabbed it again.

"I'm not going to seduce another immortal's mate." Mason rolled his eyes, "Just... try to stay still."

"If I close my eyes," I whispered. "Will I keep dreaming... things?"

Mason nodded slowly. "It's part of the process. The pain will come and go three times in the next twelve hours. You survived the first. Now you have two more."

"And Ethan?" My body shook with fear.

"Is an ass." Mason shrugged. "But I'll be here. I've seen worse, believe me. When my..." His voice died, and with it, his eyes closed. "Never mind. Just know, it will pass, and when you open your eyes, I'll be here. With water."

"And a margarita," I added, thinking that next to Ethan it sounded like the best thing in the world.

Mason burst out laughing. "I'll see what I can do." His eyes flickered to the clock by the bed. "You have five more minutes."

"You'll be here?" I asked in a weak voice.

He studied me, frowning before giving a firm nod. "I swear it."

"Thank you." I closed my eyes and lay back against the pillows, waiting for the next wave.

I expected Mason to stay put.

Instead, he lay down next to me and grabbed my hand. "You won't break me."

The last thing he whispered, "Sweet dreams," was funny because I knew that the next few hours would be nothing but nightmares and wanting something I knew I could never have.

CHAPTER NINE

Ethan

THE PAIN WAS UNBEARABLE — BECAUSE IT was a reminder of why I hated my entire existence — why I had a reason to hate.

Cassius.

Didn't it always come back to him? After all, it had started with him. Or maybe it had just started with Ara.

Another shudder wracked my body. Bones felt like they were twisting around one another before suddenly resetting themselves over and over again.

I felt her pain.

Because she was a part of me now.

So her pain was my pain.

Only for me, it was worse.

Because it was the second time in my existence I'd experienced it — when it was only supposed to be experienced once. Immortals mated for life. That was, unless someone or something intervened.

Hands shaking, I took another drink of blood. It did nothing, or maybe it did, and I was just too bitter to allow it to heal me.

She'd been naked, inconsolable, and I'd left her.

With Mason, of all creatures. My best friend, the only being other than Alex that I trusted.

My body convulsed. Falling to my knees in front of the fireplace in my room, I lifted my head to the ceiling and listened for her cries.

It was going to be a long evening.

Made longer because I'd refused to give her what she needed to make it better. I'd thought I could do it when I walked out of that room, smug as shit. I had thought I could do it.

But the pain had been too much.

The reminder.

And then the visions I'd shared with her — too personal. She'd seen Ara. She knew the shame that consumed me — or would soon know. There would be no secrets between us, and in order for the mating to continue, I had to make sure that I completely marked her, possessed her, made her mine.

It was the last thing I'd expected this morning when the number had been called.

It had been a normal day.

As normal as my life had been for the past century.

And then Cassius had breathed her name... *Genesis*. And my world stopped.

His eyes had gone completely white, and then the bastard had smirked at me, like he knew the future before the present had even happened.

It was impossible to describe the need I'd felt when I walked into that throne room. I'd heard her heartbeat on the other side of the door and had given a shaky nod to Alex, who'd seemed more amused than upset at our new circumstances.

Let Cassius have another one — and fail.

Or steal her.

Fifty years ago, I had given up my request for a breeder, as had Mason. The bond hadn't lasted like it was supposed to, and even though the bliss we'd felt at the hands of the humans we bonded with was incomparable, they'd always died.

Every. Single. Time.

And we'd been the ones left to bury them.

I could bite her and hope that she'd be the one human to finally change things.

The last one had lived past one hundred and fifty — Mason's mate. We'd thought it had worked — had thanked God.

Until he'd awoken with a corpse.

I'd already lived through enough death and betrayal, and now it seemed my existence was on repeat.

"Damn it, Ethan!" Alex stomped into the room. "Could you at least hold her hand?"

"And what? Squeeze it so hard I break every fragile bone in her pathetic body?" I hissed. "Is that what you want?"

He hung his head. "She's stronger than that."

"Is she?" I snorted out a laugh. "That's what we said about the last one."

"Who lived longer than the rest," Alex pointed out. "Look, all I'm saying is there's something very wrong about having Mason up there consoling the human when she's not even his mate, when... he may have to kill her before it's complete. I can't watch him go through loss again. He's known her for less than a day, and already he's like a kicked puppy."

"Tell him that..." I stared into the fire. "...and you'll get your throat ripped out — again."

"Once. He did that once." Alex elbowed me and took a position in front of the fire. "You did what you had to do."

"Right." My voice sounded hollow, funny, because I felt hollow, like an empty shell. "And now I'm bonded — to someone I don't love. Tell me, how does that work out in all those romance novels Stephanie likes to read?"

Alex ignored me as another one of Genesis's screams

THE DARK ONES

rocked the mansion. She was transitioning, meaning, for a human, she would be going into an absolute frenzy to be with me. I should be pleased.

I wasn't.

I wasn't that type of vampire.

One who feasted on the lust of others.

It was a trick — like magic. The mating caused her physical body to want me in ways that were indescribable, but she still had full control over her mind. And wasn't that the horrible part?

I could own her body.

I had to earn her heart.

"You're the only being alive who's pissed about having meaningless sex," Alex said in a low voice.

"Siren," I hissed, "you base your life on meaningless sex."

"And my blood pressure's way lower," he joked.

"Not laughing."

"It was kind of funny," he mumbled. "Look, just... hold her again. Maybe it will help things along. You'll sure as hell feel better. I'll sleep better. Mason won't have to kill her because she doesn't make it through, and Cassius won't end up finding her. We win."

"But do we?" I spoke the question we'd been asking ourselves for years upon years. "How long do we repeat the process? How long does the madness continue?"

Alex was silent.

Another scream.

I winced and braced myself against the mantel, nearly prying it from its place on the wall.

Alex shook his head. "If it's this bad for you — imagine how bad it is for her. She's human, Ethan. She could die. Or is that what you want? To take it all back? Would you... let her die? Just because you're afraid of what happens if she lives?"

"Take it back!" I roared; my hand crumpled the wood and tossed it into the fire.

"Fear isn't welcome here," he mocked.

I punched him in the jaw.

He went flying across the room, slamming into the wall, before chuckling and regaining his balance. "That all you got?"

"Don't tempt me to end you."

"Like you could," he spat. "Now do your job, Ethan. Go to her."

A piercing scream had me catching my breath, holding my hand to my chest.

Alex looked heavenward and swore.

"Fine," I barked. "I'll hold her — again. But you know what you ask, if that much physical contact is made? I'll be lost to her."

Alex's smile fell from his face. "You've been lost to her from the minute Cassius uttered her name. Don't for one second think otherwise. Now go to her, before you give her to Cassius like before."

"Leave," I barked. "And never speak of that again."

Alex held up his hands and stomped out of the room.

While my heart decided to ram against my ribs so hard I had to fight to catch a breath again.

Slowly, I made my way up to her room. The screams were getting louder and louder, but the closer my body was the less the pain.

Finally, when I entered the room, it was to see Mason pacing a hole through the damn floor and pulling at his overly long hair.

"Leave us," I whispered in a hoarse voice.

Mason paused, tilted his head, and smirked, "Careful, humans do break."

"I can be gentle."

He barked out a laugh. "You drove your fist into a granite countertop when we ran out of wine last week."

I rolled my eyes and pointed to the door.

CHAPTER TEN

Genesis

COOL WATER TOUCHED MY LIPS. GREEDILY, I reached out, my hands coming into contact with the glass and something else warm. I drank as much as I could and then slowly opened my eyes.

Ethan.

My heart clenched in my chest. Was he back to make fun of me? Watch me suffer only to leave again? I recoiled, the pain started to subside enough that I didn't want to actually kill myself.

Apparently, I'd asked Mason to do just that a few times.

"Sorry..." Ethan mumbled, setting the glass down on the table. "If I stay, it will be... easier."

It didn't feel easier.

It felt hot.

Not exactly painful, but hot to the point that my body kept telling me if I only scooted a little bit closer to him, I'd be okay. If only he'd tilt his head a fraction of an inch and kiss me — the pain would dissipate completely. I was at war with my own body, and I hated him for causing it — for bonding with me without even asking if it was okay first.

Not that I'd had a lot of options once my number had been called.

And once Cassius had marked me.

I'd dreamt of him again.

Of his cool lips. I'd reached out, but the minute my hands had come into contact with his body, I'd been jolted awake by Mason.

His words had been clear. *"Never, under any circumstances touch Cassius."* Even in my dreams.

Weird.

A shudder wracked my body. Ethan let out a curse then wrapped his arm around me. His skin was hot to the touch, but it still comforted me. I ducked my head under his arm and let out a heavy sigh as another wave of pain shot from my toes all the way up to my head, causing a splitting headache.

I turned into his body — not really in control of my own actions — just knowing that he would make it better.

He shifted next to me, pulling me closer.

"So..." His voice was hoarse. "Tell me about... school."

"What?" I gasped, my voice sounded like I'd spent the night screaming at a concert. "School?"

"Yeah, your studies... about immortals. Tell me about it."

"Immortals suck." I sighed. "If I disrespect you enough, will you kill me?"

His lips twitched as if he was fighting a smile. "Not now, no. It would be like killing myself."

"And that's supposed to deter me from wanting certain death?"

This time he did smile. "What did you learn about mating?"

"There was no mating chapter." My hand pressed against his chest. What was I doing? My fingers ducked into the *V* of his white shirt, pressing against his warm skin. I wanted to taste him. Why?

"Hmm…" His free hand moved to cover mine and slowly peel it from his body. "That's unfortunate."

"Yeah." I jerked my hand away from his and placed it against his skin again. It felt too good, and I was so sick and tired of feeling pain.

He hissed out a breath and closed his eyes, leaning his head back against the headboard. "You have one more transition before the bond is complete. Your body will crave mine… but it doesn't have to mean anything."

"Huh?" I was too distracted by the curve of his full mouth to hear all the words coming out of it. His lips were so full and inviting. I leaned forward.

Ethan kept my body pinned so I couldn't move. The more I squirmed against him the more irritated he looked. His eyes were so green and captivating it seemed like they were glowing.

"Not this way," he whispered. "When you come to me… fully as yourself. When your love for me and only me blots out any sort of physical need you have — that's when I'll give in."

"And if that never happens?" I fought against him; I just wanted a taste, and I didn't even like him. It made no sense.

He shrugged. "Wouldn't be the first time."

I closed my eyes and tried to focus on the pain rather than on him… because when I focused on him, I hated myself a little bit more.

"Questions—" he choked out. "I know you have questions… so ask."

"Can't…" I shook my head. His voice was so pretty, so deep. What would it feel like to be with him? Just once. He'd make the pain go away; he'd make everything better. If I could just touch him more, taste him. My body strained toward his. "I can't stop thinking about you."

"Flattered," he said dryly. "Try."

"But—"

"Favorite color."

"What?" My eyes jerked open. "Did you just ask me my favorite color?"

He smirked. "Tell me it's green."

I rolled my eyes, some of the need dying a bit at his arrogance. "White."

His nostrils flared. "Cassius would be pleased."

"Not because of Cassius," I said in a soft voice. "Because white's like a blank slate. It means starting over."

"You wish..." He swallowed, his head tilting to the side, pieces of dark hair falling across his sculpted face. "...to start over?"

"I wish I would have run..." My body trembled as more heat invaded my stomach. "...when they called my number."

His smile made my stomach clench. "You can't run from destiny."

"I could have tried."

"You would have failed," he said in amused tone. "And you would have most likely died at Cassius's hand for trying."

"Why did he mark me? How did he mark me?"

Ethan sighed. "His touch... if he touches any part of you, it marks you. He has to will it to happen, so it's a switch he can turn on and off. All of the Dark Ones can. He touched your shoulder, infused your body. It never takes much from a Dark One. They're... powerful."

I nodded my head, remembering the sting of cold that hit me when Cassius had touched my shoulder. "And the only way to take the marking away?"

"Is to cover it up." Ethan clenched his teeth. "Or in this case... infuse you with my essence."

"Your essence is strong enough to do that?" My teeth clenched together in pain. The heat from my stomach had traveled to my mouth. I eyed the water greedily.

Ethan lifted it to my lips. "Only if I'm without a mate..."

I sipped the liquid and took a breath. "You had a mate."

"Had," Ethan repeated.

I didn't push him; if there was one thing I'd learned, it was that when his eyes glowed, it wasn't because he was in a particularly happy mood. Water dripped from my chin; he caught it with his fingertip and brought it to his lips.

"You taste..." He closed his eyes. "...heavenly."

"Did you bite me?" I blurted.

He dropped his finger from his mouth and smirked. "You'd know if I bit you."

"So what did you do?"

"Shared my blood with you... the old fashioned way. With a knife."

"But wouldn't it have been easier to—"

"Biting is too personal," he finished, "intimate... not something shared with strangers."

"Or humans?" I asked.

"Or that."

"But Mason bit me."

"Mason has a different way of doing things, and, not that it matters, but his bite wasn't one of mating. It was done to try to cover up Cassius's mark, nothing more."

"So..." I pulled myself away from him; I was starting to get too hot again. "You've saved me... to what end?"

Ethan's eyes turned very serious as he whispered, "Hopefully, one day... you'll be able to return the favor. And save us."

CHAPTER ELEVEN

Ethan

HER EYEBROWS DREW TOGETHER IN WHAT I could only assume was frustration. Her heart started to race, and then her eyes dilated as she glanced at my mouth again. If she did that one more time, I was going to lose my mind. I was already trying desperately to keep her from touching me too much. Because it affected me, as much as I wanted to deny it, to deny her.

Her physical contact was everything I'd been craving.

Giving in would be easy.

Staying away would be hard.

But traveling down that road again — knowing how it was likely to end — well, I wasn't so sure I would survive it. I was immortal, but my heart was still fragile.

And when it broke...

As in immortal, I suffered with unimaginable pain. Pain I never wanted to experience again, thus the reason for keeping myself firmly tucked away from the weak little human with the pretty smile.

I liked her hair.

It was gold, not really brown, not blond — just gold. The

firelight made certain pieces glow. It was tempting to grab it, to sniff it, to wrap it around my fingers and imagine what she'd be like in the throes of passion.

"Ethan..." My name on her lips was ecstasy. I shook the thought away and tried to appear indifferent.

"Yes?"

"I can't save anyone... I can't even save myself."

"You're stronger than you think," I encouraged. "Trust me."

"That's just it." She tugged her lower lip into her mouth and chewed, her dark blue eyes sad. "You've given me no reason to."

"You're alive," I pointed out. "That's reason enough."

"He's not the best at comforting humans," came Alex's voice from the door. I could hear the amusement in his tone.

I rolled my eyes and turned, ready to bark at him to leave.

"Cassius called," Alex said in a bored tone. "Wanted to know if I know where the human is."

"And?"

"I lied." Alex rolled his eyes. "Of course."

"And he didn't believe you?"

"Naturally." Alex examined his fingernails and shrugged. "So I told him you'd trapped her in your lair and were having your way with her."

Genesis let out a little whimper and ran her hands down my chest again.

I clenched my teeth and hissed out a breath. "Could we not discuss this now?"

Alex held up his hands. "Just thought you should know... he isn't pleased that you've bonded with her. I lied and said it was complete."

"He'll still try to take her, regardless." I licked my lips and tried to focus on Alex rather than the fact that Genesis was drawing circles on my chest, making me want to lean into her, capture her lips and suck.

"Yup." Alex grinned as he watched the scene in front of him like it was some hilarious movie and not my life. "So, this looks cozy."

"Was there anything else?" I barked.

"Complete the mating." He nodded. "At least then her eyes will be opened fully... and we can see if this was all worth it."

Genesis let out a moan. Heat shot through my body, slicing me nearly in half. She was transitioning into the final phase.

Alex had the good sense to look like he felt sorry for her before nodding his head again and shutting the door.

"Please!" Genesis begged, gripping my shirt with both of her hands. Her eyes rolled to the back of her head. "Make it stop, please! It's so hot."

It was about to get worse.

The final stage always was.

Like taking knives from a fire and slicing up your body. I'd always been told that during this stage, humans dreamt of Death.

And because of that fact, Death visited them, beckoned them, and many, took his outstretched hand and never woke up.

"Listen..." I cupped her face with my hands. "...focus on me... not the pain. It's almost over."

"And you'll be here?" Her body started to convulse as my blood merged with hers. The same blood I'd shared with her when I'd marked her. "P-promise?"

"Yes."

Her eyes flashed green, mimicking mine.

"I won't leave your side."

"My mouth..." She shook her head violently, her lips swollen from the heat. "...hurts."

I pressed my mouth to hers gently and then pierced the skin of her upper lip, relieving the pressure of the blood in her system — my blood fighting hers as it should, her blood refusing to give up as it should.

Humans always tasted the same — like life — like earth mixed with sugar. It was addicting. I'd always thought it was too sweet.

But she tasted perfect.

"More..." She tugged at my shirt again.

I kissed her again, this time slanting my mouth over where my fangs had dug into her tender skin.

I was old.

Able to control myself.

At least that was what I said when I kissed her a third time, this time more passionately. And when she clung to me like I was her only chance at survival, I wanted to roar with excitement. It was the bond.

Nothing more.

I kissed her harder.

Her nails dug into my skin.

"Fight it, Genesis." I was speaking to myself as much as I was to her. I needed to fight it too... because I knew firsthand there was nothing worse than mating with someone, wanting someone so badly, and thinking it was love.

And realizing it was nothing but a very pretty lie.

Her head dropped back, exposing her full neck.

Sweat dripped from her face down her neck as another stab of pain hit me and her in the chest.

She was fighting it.

But she was also fighting me.

She had spirit.

I only hoped that when death visited her in her dreams, she wouldn't take his cold lifeless hand.

Because maybe I could never love her. Maybe she could never love me. But I respected her strength.

And in all my years — I was beginning to think maybe it was time to have a friend I could at least share the loneliness with.

A real mate.

She screamed.

And blacked out.

I pulled her into my lap and kissed her forehead. She moved against me and then stopped.

Her body went ice cold.

Death was visiting.

All I could do was wait.

CHAPTER TWELVE

Genesis

I FELT ETHAN NEXT TO ME. I wanted to ask him what was happening next, why my body was suddenly cold — why everything felt numb — but I couldn't open my eyes.

I was trapped in darkness.

"So," a low whispery voice spoke into the darkness, "will you stay or will you go?"

"What?" I spoke into the darkness, unable to see anything around me. White smoke suddenly appeared in front of me, and then a hand reached out through the smoke.

"Will you come with me? Allow me to ease all your pain? Or will you stay?"

The hand looked so welcoming.

The closer it came to my body the more I wanted to take it.

But I could still feel Ethan, and leaving him... felt so wrong. My body shuddered at the thought.

"Choose," the voice commanded.

I didn't want to choose. I just wanted to go back to my normal existence, where I went to Starbucks in the mornings and did homework in the afternoons.

Those days were long gone.

"Choose," it said, louder this time.

I swayed toward the hand.

But something held me back.

The pain flared again — unbearable — as if someone had stabbed me in the heart.

"I can take it all away," the voice soothed. "Just take my hand."

Was I crazy? To choose the pain over this man's hand? Over what I was sure would be complete and total peace?

Ethan meant pain.

And as much as I hated him in that instant — I needed him... even if it meant pain.

It was his eyes.

They reflected what I felt in my own body — in my soul.

He was suffering, just like me, only it was a different kind of suffering, one that I'm sure had to do with the vision I'd seen of him and the woman.

"Choose!" the voice boomed.

I stepped backward and wrapped my hands around my body. "Him. I choose him."

The cloud disappeared, revealing a man who looked a lot like Cassius. I wasn't sure if he was a Dark One, but the air around him seemed to freeze in place. I shivered.

His eyes flashed white.

So he was a Dark One.

His teeth were shaped like tiny knives.

"It won't be easy," he spoke softly, "choosing life."

"It shouldn't be easy..." I found my voice. "...to choose death."

He smiled, bowed his head, and disappeared.

The pain in my chest spread to my back. I arched, and then everything stopped. The pain, the heat, my heart slowed.

And I blinked my eyes open.

Ethan hovered over me in a shielding stance, almost like he was protecting me from someone coming into the room and knifing me in my sleep. His eyes were black.

"I..." My voice sounded groggy, foreign to my ears. "I think it's done."

His eyes slowly faded to gray and then green. "You chose me." His voice cracked.

"Well..." I licked my lips, just looking at his mouth at my body, yearning for his touch. "It was either you or the guy with the creepy voice."

Ethan's delicious mouth broke out into a smile. "Does that mean you don't find me creepy?"

I examined the fangs protruding over his plump lips. "You're a different kind of creepy."

He leaned back on his knees and pulled me up so I was in a sitting position. "Didn't think you'd wake up spouting compliments and poetry." He sighed. "It's almost complete."

"Almost?" I croaked. "I have to go through more pain?"

"No..." His eyes flashed. "...just pleasure."

"Wha—"

His mouth was on my neck before I had a chance to utter any more words. His tongue twisted and pushed against the base of my throat.

I bucked off the bed as a sweet sensation of euphoria washed over me.

When he pulled back, his eyes were so bright green it hurt to stare directly at him. "Now that... was me biting you."

"Yeah..." I managed to push the word past my stunned lips. "It was."

He moved off the bed at epic speed and was already at the door when I blinked for a second time. "Stephanie will be in to help you shower and dress. We'll discuss your... duties... when you've regained some of your strength."

"Wait!" I blurted.

He paused at the door, his hands digging into the wood. "Yes?"

"Am I still human?"

He burst out laughing and turned. "Of course... still weak,

still fragile, still very much... human."

"Oh..." I nodded, my studies of vampires were clearly lacking since I'd learned that a bite could turn you or worse, kill you. "...that's good, right?"

"Depends on who you ask, I suppose." He shrugged and shut the door softly behind him.

I was too tired to focus on what that cryptic sentence may have meant and didn't have time to mull it over like I typically would because Stephanie burst through that same door two minutes later yelling, "You lived!"

Did that mean she'd thought I would die?

"Good for you." She nodded. "Things are finally looking up!" She clapped her hands and dropped a set of clothes onto the nearby chair. "Let's get you showered and looking your best so you can start producing little vampire babies."

I felt my stomach drop. "Wh-what?"

"It was a joke." She winked. "Well, the vampire babies part. Now, let's get you feeling better. I'll have Alex in here a bit later to stabilize you and—"

"Stabilize me?" I repeated. "What?"

"It's what he does." She nodded. "He's a siren — makes girls feel calm when all they want to do is pull their hair out and scream. I'd do it, but it only works on men... thus the need for him to do it. Don't worry though. It's like taking a Xanax, only it feels way better."

"I don't want to feel drugged," I mumbled, my body aching in places I didn't know even existed. "I think right now I just want a shower."

Stephanie shifted on her feet. "He didn't hurt you... did he?"

Well, my physical body was intact, but my heart was really confused. Did it hurt? No, but something felt wrong. Like I should be happy, elated even, rather than depressed and rejected.

"No," I finally answered. "I'm great."

"Good." She exhaled. "Now, about that shower."

CHAPTER THIRTEEN

Ethan

I STILL TASTED HER BLOOD ON my lips, was embarrassed for the first time in a century when Alex glanced up from his spot at the kitchen table to see me licking my lips like I'd just devoured the poor girl.

He shook his head. "Been that long, huh?"

"Alex..." I closed my eyes and prayed for patience. "...remind me why I let you live here?"

"I'm good-looking," he answered simply. "Besides, I'm a hell of a fighter — scrappy, I think is how you define my kind. You need me."

"Stop." I pressed my fingertips to my temples and rubbed. The ache to have her had consumed me so much that I'd run down the stairs moving so fast I'd nearly collided with a wall, and grabbed blood from the fridge.

I didn't need it.

But I craved it.

And if I didn't drink the donated blood, I sure as hell was going to drain her and enjoyed very last drop.

"I wonder..." Alex's voice pierced my thoughts. "What's it

like?" He leaned forward. "Having to learn self-control all over again... being as ancient as you are?"

I ignored him.

He kept talking.

"Blood-free for a century and now..." He grinned and licked his lips. "Kind of like falling off the wagon, yeah?"

"You're giving me a headache." I threw the empty bag of blood at his face. He moved to the side and snickered. "And I'm fine. Everything is just—"

Her smell was intoxicating. She was walking down the stairs, so her heart picked up speed, her body giving off a scent of burnt vanilla and oranges with a hint of sugar. My mouth literally watered.

"Fine?" Alex said in a mocking voice. "Was that what you were going to say? Damn, man show a little decorum, you look... starved."

"I am," I whispered and fought the urge to rock back and forth. That was the problem with mating — with bonding. Nothing tasted like her, nothing ever would, and typically, having her as my mate gave me full access.

But the more I took...

The stronger the bond.

And the more I wanted...

It was a vicious overwhelming cycle. It would lead me to become emotionally invested while she, as a human, could simply pretend.

It wasn't fair.

Immortals, in essence, were cursed with a deep desire to be like a human — to possess them, to bond with them forever — while humans only felt the same draw to us if they actually loved us.

Ridiculous.

"Oh, there you are." Stephanie pushed Genesis forward and pulled out a chair.

Slowly, Genesis took a seat and glared at each one of us.

"Where's Mason?"

It shouldn't have pissed me off.

But it had.

"He's none of your concern," I spat.

"Easy!" Alex chuckled. "Rule number one, don't ask your mate where the other dude is. Just... don't."

Genesis blinked at Alex then back at me. "Because you guys have the capacity for jealousy."

Alex whistled while Stephanie laughed.

Immortals were the most jealous beings on the planet. Had her school taught her nothing?

Was I to be her tutor as well?

"So..." Alex trained his eyes on her, putting her at as much ease as he could without stopping her poor heart. "Now that the mating is complete, you get to learn all about us and service your man here." He slapped my back.

Really. Really. Poor choice of words.

Genesis paled.

I rolled my eyes. "He's kidding."

Alex laughed. "I think it needs to be said that having a human at the house has already helped my mood immensely."

"That makes one of you," Genesis said under her breath.

Alex leaned forward and whispered, "Ethan, try not to be so grouchy. Keep the fangs in and all."

I extended them just to prove a point.

Genesis recoiled.

I instantly felt guilty.

Damn it.

"You won't..." I licked my lips. "You won't have to service me, as Alex so delicately put it."

"Is that what mates do?" Genesis asked, her eyes searching mine. "They..." She lifted her hands into the air and dropped them.

"If that's what you think they do, we have a very big problem." Alex mimicked her movements and winked.

She blushed.

I hissed at him and returned my attention to her. "It's like a human relationship, only stronger. You'll attend functions with me, be by my side, at my beck and call for as long as you live."

I didn't want to say until one day she just didn't wake up. It sounded too cruel.

"And when I'm bored out of my mind... I do what?" She crossed her arms. "I mean, what could you possibly need from me?"

"Adorable." Alex sighed happily. "I'm so glad we kept her."

"Alex..." I was two seconds away from slamming him into the nearest wall. "Make yourself useful and find our human a snack."

"I'm not a pet!" Genesis yelled. "And I'm not your human!"

"You are," I yelled right back, "mine!"

"Kids." Stephanie stepped between us.

I didn't even realize I'd gotten out of the chair and was towering over her, fangs out, hands raised. She'd turned me into a monster. And still, my eyes found her erratic pulse. One more taste...

"Ethan—" Stephanie pushed against my chest. I didn't move. "Ethan!"

"Friend..." Mason walked into the room. "Sit your ass down before she hands it to you."

"Like she could!" I roared.

"Like I have!" Stephanie pushed me again. "Don't tempt me... again."

I sat, while Mason made his way over to Genesis and offered an easy smile. The man had nothing to smile about, yet he was smiling — at my mate.

I growled.

Mason gave me the finger and kept his attention trained

on Genesis. "How do you feel?"

"Better." She returned his smile and squeezed his outstretched hand. "Thanks for not... killing me when I asked."

"Damn..." Alex said from the kitchen.

"You were in pain." Mason shrugged. "And I'm glad you're alright."

"She's fine. We're fine. Everything's fine," I said through clenched teeth. "Now it's probably time to give her answers before she thinks she can run off and actually survive in the real world without being hunted by a Dark One, or worse, found by Cassius."

"He isn't all bad," Stephanie said defensively.

We all glared at her.

"What?" She lifted her hands into the air. "I'm just saying he's been trying as hard as we have. So what if he's gotten a bit possessive over the last few numbers that have been called."

Alex slammed his fist onto the table. "He stole Ethan's—"

"Enough." I held up my hand. The pain in my chest grew until it was hard to breathe. I knew what would take that pain away.

Genesis.

But I was too angry to ask for it. To ashamed to fall to my knees in front of a mere mortal and beg for her to end the pain by allowing me one solitary drop of her blood.

As if on cue, another bag of blood hit me in the head.

Alex must have sensed my mood.

I bit into it and looked away from Genesis's horrified expression.

"Lesson time." Alex placed some fruit and cheese in front of Genesis and clapped his hands. "Who goes first?"

Nobody said anything.

Genesis cleared her throat. "Maybe if you'll start by telling me what our real job is... as human breeders. All my life I've been taught a lie and now... well, now I'd really like to know how this all started and what my place is."

Overwhelming her with information just might kill her. It would be like telling a child that her existence was simply for the pleasure of the parent, that she meant nothing in the grand scheme of things.

"The numbers," Mason cleared his throat, "have been called for centuries. It used to be every year, then it went to every two years, every decade — you know the trend. The last human number called was fifty years ago." His face contorted like he was going to change shape, but he gained control over himself. "Immortals, as we've said before, cannot simply procreate. They need humans in order for the process to be complete. Basically, human men and women help immortals continue to populate the planet. If the balance is somehow... broken, then chaos erupts, thus the need for humans. The balance is very important for both our races."

"Okay." Genesis, nodded her head slowly. "So why wait fifty years?"

You could hear a pin drop in that room.

I didn't want to answer.

Mason kicked me under the table. I glowered in his direction then said as gently as I could, "Because immortals become attached to their humans in a very... possessive way. They mate for life... it's a beautiful thing, but the human always has the choice to reject their mate." *Even after they've bonded*, but I wasn't going to say that aloud lest she reject me. "If the mating is completed, both parties happy, babies are born into the world, and everyone lives happily ever after — that's fantastic, but recently, humans started... dying."

"That's what we generally do." Genesis's eyes narrowed. "We don't live forever."

"After giving birth to an immortal, you should. You used to." Mason explained. "It's life's final gift... immortality for your sacrifice to us. But somehow, along the way, it stopped working."

"Oh." Genesis glanced at me.

I looked away. Not wanting her to see my pain.

"And how does Cassius fit into all of this?" she asked.

"The Dark Ones don't mate. They don't bond in the way we do. When they infuse a human mate, it's too strong for the humans to handle it, but he was... or we were... for a while, experimenting with the idea. Thinking we were possibly losing our powers. He's been taking humans... to see if he can reverse it, but along the way he became..." I sighed. "...addicted."

"What?" Genesis shook her head. "To what exactly?"

"He's part angel... part human," Mason said in a low voice. "His human counterpart wants desperately to join with humanity again — but his angelic essence won't let him. He's stuck in hell. But when a Dark One infuses a human, for those blissful weeks they last, life is perfect. Cassius is convinced if he only found the right human, he could bond eternally."

"And that was me?" Genesis croaked. "Or he thought it was me?"

Because of her marking.

Because of her name.

The beginning. Her name meant the beginning. And our prophecies specifically stated that a woman's number would be called who represented a fresh start.

A new beginning.

Cassius wanted her for his own selfish reasons.

The rest of the immortals wanted her so mates would stop dying, children would no longer be motherless or fatherless.

I kept my groan inside. It was even harder for the men. The minute they bonded with an immortal woman their original chemical makeup ceased to exist, relying solely on their immortal wives for nutrients, their organs simply started shutting down only days after the bond was complete.

I wanted to believe my own reasons weren't selfish.

But with each breath she took, each beat of her heart, I realized I was more selfish than Cassius, because, as of right now, I wouldn't give her up — even if it meant war. Even if it meant the end of my own people — my existence.

For being as old as I was, retraining myself wasn't going to be easy. Keeping emotional barriers between us would be necessary because my body screamed for her.

CHAPTER FOURTEEN

Genesis

WORDS DIDN'T HAVE POWER, RIGHT? THEY were just words, strung together in sentences, big scary sentences that had me shaking. I wondered when or if the fear would ever leave.

I stared at the fruit on the table, not in the least bit hungry.

"I can't just..." I found my voice and glanced up at Ethan. "I can't just sit around trapped in this house away from the world. It would be like prison."

"A beautiful prison." Ethan smiled.

I chose not to smile back. I didn't want to encourage him or encourage my body to lean any closer to his. His body was like a magnet, even if I fought against the pull — I still couldn't help it. I found myself inching my chair closer. When it scraped against the floor, everyone smirked but Ethan.

He seemed angry.

Angry, yet he'd been the one to do that to me.

"I don't care," I said, ignoring the thumping of my heart in my chest and the fact that the closer I got to him the more it raced. "I can't just sit around here being worthless."

"You won't," Stephanie piped up. "Your life will be

relatively normal. Ethan can even get you a job if you want... close by... so he can keep an eye on you, of course."

"A job?"

"Work," Ethan said slowly. "Isn't that what humans live for? A divine purpose? Though, if you'd rather stay here cook and clean, you won't get any complaints."

"A job would be nice." Anything to get me out of the house or compound.

"Fantastic," Ethan said, his teeth snapping together.

I had a sinking feeling it was anything but fantastic, but I wasn't about to bend over backward and let him make yet another decision for me — regardless of how much I wanted to launch myself at him and never let go.

It was the bond.

Nothing more.

And that really sucked if you asked me, because someone like Ethan... well, he was the type of man, person, being that you wanted to want you. Not just because he had no choice, but because he couldn't imagine existing any other way.

Ashamed of my thoughts — or maybe just embarrassed — I returned to my stare-down with the kitchen table.

"Drystan owns a book shop," Stephanie suggested. "When Genesis isn't with us fighting crime, she can go there. God knows she'll need to get away from Ethan in order to have some breathing room."

Ethan rolled his eyes.

"Drystan?" I repeated. "He's immortal too?"

"Ancient." Mason nodded. "Another werewolf obsessed with books. It should be a good arrangement."

"Arrangement," I tested the word. "And when I'm not at the book shop?"

The others fell silent while Ethan reached across the table and grabbed my hand. My skin buzzed to life at his touch. "I teach you everything you need to know about us... about your job, about the humans' place with us... and I take you to your first Gathering."

"Like a party?" I gripped his hand tighter, pulling strength from him that I didn't know I needed but lusted for, nonetheless.

"Yes." He shrugged. "In fact, if you're up to it, we can introduce you this evening."

"Oh." Waves of pleasure washed over me as he released my hand; his fingertips dancing along the pulse in my wrist. "I think I can probably manage that."

"The others will love to meet you," Stephanie encouraged, placing her hands on my shoulders.

"How many others are we talking here?" I squinted. "In my studies it said that the oldest leaders... you guys..."

Alex choked on his laugh.

"...only number in the hundreds."

The laughter died, amusement gone from Alex's eyes.

"Four of us," Ethan answered. "There are four Elders left, and Cassius makes five. The rest are relatively younger, but they number in the thousands."

"For just Seattle?" I squeaked out.

"Of course." Ethan rolled his eyes and released my hand. The temperature in the room dipped. My hand itched to reach back and grasp his. "Immortals are able to live in society, you know. Most of us either have a job in the real world or have had in the past until it began to bore us."

"Weird, I was always told you kept to yourselves."

"We aren't good at keeping to ourselves, just like we aren't good with sharing." Alex grinned. "Isn't that right, Ethan?"

Ethan growled while Alex walked around the table and held out his hand. "Has anyone ever told you how beautiful you truly are? It's extraordinary... the color of your hair, the light of your eyes, the—"

Ethan kicked Alex in the back of the legs, sending him colliding into Stephanie. His laughter was the only thing that made me think that Ethan wasn't going to kill him, since his eyes had gone completely black.

"Need more blood?" Alex asked in a soothing tone. "Don't want you accidentally attacking your mate tonight in front of God and everyone."

My gut clenched. "Do you, um, take my blood?"

"Please." Alex laughed. "Like Ethan would... he's been celibate from blood for over a hundred years."

"Until now," I whispered.

Ethan looked away, his eyes getting blacker, if that was even possible. "Until I tasted you."

A small part of me hoped I tasted good to him.

Oh you do, came Alex's voice in my head. *Like pure sin.*

I felt my cheeks heat.

Ethan's eyes narrowed. "Stephanie, help Genesis get ready for this evening... keep her occupied while I go meet with Cassius."

"What?" I yelled. "You're going to meet with him? After what happened? After going to all this trouble to protect me?"

"Hear that?" Alex cupped his ear. "Her blood roars for you, Ethan."

Ethan seemed to focus on my mouth as his fangs descended over his bottom lip. Holy crap, was he going to bite me again? My breathing slowed.

His eyes went from black to green then back to black again as he cupped the back of my head and brought me close, his teeth grazing my neck.

With a hiss, he pushed me away, almost hard enough for my chair to topple backward if Stephanie hadn't caught it with her hands.

"Go," he said in a hoarse voice, "before I drain her."

I didn't need to be told twice that it was dangerous just being next to him. I bolted from my seat, ready to protect myself, if need be, when Mason moved to stand in front of me, bumping against Ethan's chest. "Not necessary to scare her shitless, vampire."

Ethan looked over Mason's shoulder, his body calling to mine, singing, beckoning, even though he was dangerous, even though he'd just threatened me, I wanted to push Mason out of the way more than I wanted air.

"Take care of her," Ethan barked. "I won't be long."

"Stay alive," Alex said in a cheerful voice. "And do tell Cassius hello."

Stephanie put a protective arm around me and whispered in my ear. "It will get better, you know. He's just angry and confused."

"And I'm not?" I wrapped my arms around myself. "This morning I woke up, and the only thing on my mind was if I wanted eggs for breakfast or a protein shake."

"And now," Alex offered with a slight shrug, "you get to worry about two immortals wanting your blood. No big, right?"

"Is that you trying to make me feel better?"

"No..." He smiled. "But this is." His blue eyes lit up just as Mason shoved him out of the way and Stephanie began tugging me back up the stairs.

"He's insane, but I love him." She shook her head. "Now, let's get you ready for this evening. I think I'll put you in red. Won't that drive Ethan absolutely wild?"

"I'm thinking Ethan needs no encouragement to end me," I grumbled.

Stephanie pushed open the door to another room, one I hadn't seen before. "He doesn't want to end you. He wants to drink from you — so much, in fact, that I'm pretty sure if he doesn't regain some focus, he's going to punch Cassius in the face."

"That can't end well."

"They fight." She shrugged. "Quite often."

"Isn't Cassius your... king?" I was going to try to find a better word, but that was the only one that seemed to fit.

"Somewhat." She looked down at the ground. "Or at least at one point, he was supposed to lead us — but it's hard, for an imperfect being, pulled between two mortal planes, to do that without losing himself in the process."

"What do you mean?"

"He's both human and immortal. He has two different types of chemical makeup fighting for dominance. Sometimes his human side wins. Other times, the angel side. It's frustrating to follow someone who doesn't even know himself."

"Hmm." I thought about that for a while; they'd made me believe Cassius was like Satan himself, but now I was starting to wonder if he was just misunderstood.

"When you close your eyes," she whispered under her breath, "he'll explain himself better."

"Who?"

"Cassius."

"What? Did I miss an important part of this conversation?"

"You'll see." She smiled. "And then you can make your own judgment, yes?"

"Um, sure?"

"Yes, this!" She moved to a large closet and opened the doors. "I think the dress is in here."

I was still mulling over the fact that Cassius would somehow explain himself to me when a shoe flew by my head, missing my cheek by mere inches. I flinched.

"Sorry! I forget you're breakable."

"Very." I paid special attention to flying objects and went over to the closet. "Will Cassius be there tonight?"

"If Ethan allows it."

"And he won't try to take me."

"Not with us there, no."

"But he'll still try."

Stephanie's hand hovered over the other shoe. "Every day.

Until you no longer exist."

CHAPTER FIFTEEN

Ethan

I SHOULD HAVE KNOWN SOMETHING WAS wrong the minute I got into my new Lexus LFA and drove like hell down the winding road.

I'd become accustomed to nice things in life. Living as long as I had, I'd learned to take pleasure from hobbies. My interests ranged from collecting fine art to archery. Had I not done something with my time I would have gone absolutely insane.

My most recent pleasure? Cars. The leather felt smooth against my hot skin; the smell tantalized me. And the speed? Well, the speed was just a bonus. But not now... it seemed everything absolutely paled in comparison to the taste of her.

Maybe it had been too long — the effects of bloodlust could drive a vampire insane — but it wasn't mindless lust I was feeling for her, just intense desire to be near her, to drink from her, to share my soul with her for no other reason than I'd bonded with her.

But if I shared more of my blood, if I took more from her, giving her mine in exchange, she'd continue to be able to see my memories, my dreams — everything I'd been keeping close for the past hundred years.

And the horrible part? She wasn't invested, at least not emotionally, and the last thing I wanted was for her to pity me. The idea made me snort out loud, a human pitying an immortal. The idea was laughable, if it wasn't so damn tragic.

She'd want to make the pain go away…

When really I just wanted to start over.

Cassius wasn't at his usual spot, opting for a more public arena. I hadn't wanted to argue with him yet again over what his presence did to mere mortals. I'd simply sent him a text and agreed to meet in the U District for coffee.

Cassius hated coffee.

But he drank it because it made him feel normal.

I drank it because it took the edge off wanting to rip someone's throat out.

The car squealed into a nearby parking spot. I hit the alarm and made my way toward Starbucks.

People stared.

They couldn't help it.

Just like they couldn't help but ask for autographs, even though they had no idea who I was — just assumed, by my looks, that I was famous or about to be.

Years ago, it had been flattering — when I still possessed a heart and didn't think the world was going to come crashing down around me at any second. Years ago, I had been naïve.

No more.

Cassius was sitting outside, though it was drizzling. He was covered by the umbrella, sipping at his cappuccino and reading the freaking newspaper, like he didn't already know everything there was to know.

I dropped my keys onto the table loudly.

He didn't look up. "Got you a caramel-macchiato thing that tastes like hell. You're welcome."

Rolling my eyes, I took the cup into my hands and sat

down, bringing the hot liquid to my mouth.

It was bitter.

It tasted nothing like her.

I couldn't even pretend that I was enjoying myself. Would nothing take the edge off?

"So..." Cassius set down the paper, and gazed at me from behind his sunglasses, which kept people from asking why the hell his eyes kept turning white. "That was clever of you."

"Vampires... we're known for it," I said in a dry tone, leaning back in my chair. "Besides, you owed me, and you know it."

"I saved your life." Cassius snorted. "I hardly think that puts me in your debt."

"You had no proof, no right, no—"

He held up his hand. "Enough. I don't wish to discuss the past."

He never did.

I cursed and took another sip of coffee. "What's done is done. Now we wait."

Cassius looked so out of place sitting in a small chair, appearing to fit in. His body was too large, his countenance too dangerous. He tilted his head as if listening to the wind. "Her scent is on you."

"Caught that, did you?"

"A hundred years."

"People really need to stop reminding me," I grumbled, no longer interested in my coffee or the conversation we were having. Why the hell I'd agreed to meet with someone I used to call brother was beyond me.

"You aren't as strong as I am, Ethan. You cannot hope to keep me from her, not when so much is at stake."

And there it was.

I hissed out a breath. "I'm afraid your hands are tied."

"Are they?"

I stood, placing my palms on the table, towering over

everyone. "You'd repeat history for your own selfish reasons? Is that what this is? I'm trying to save lives, Cassius! This has nothing to do with her!"

"Which is why your eyes," he said calmly, "continue to go black, why your blood boils beneath the skin that covers it, why your heart is in perfect cadence with hers. Yes, I can hear it, even from this far away, though I can't directly find her. Know this... I will."

"Unless you get her alone, you have no chance." I sat, half-tempted to toss my coffee in his face and tear his throat out for good measure.

"She'll come to me of her own accord. When you fail — and fail you will — she'll come to me. They always do."

My body shuddered with the onslaught of past memories. "You brainwashed her."

"I offered her a solution."

"You gave her death."

"I didn't say it was a good solution." Cassius shrugged. "Remember this, I've been damned to earth to help your cause — to help the immortals and humans keep balance. When you fail, it's my head — not yours."

I rolled my eyes. "It's been over five-hundred years since we've had a visit from one of the archangels. I highly doubt they're going to do it now. There's nothing special about her." That was a lie.

"I smell your doubt, vampire." Cassius growled my name pushed back the chair and stood. "Have your fun, try to win her affection, but know in the end, it will be me who has to save everyone."

"Has anyone ever told you that you have a god-complex?"

"I come by that quite naturally, I assure you." He nodded and walked off, calling behind him, "Do your worst, Ethan, or maybe I should say...try your best?"

"Ah, so may the best man win and all of that." I laughed. "Yet you forget. Your very essence will kill her."

"We don't know that for sure." He raised one hand and lifted the opposite shoulder in a seemingly casual shrug. "And I'm willing to take that risk. In order to save us all, I would take that risk every time. I wonder... would you?"

I swallowed and looked away, knowing he'd hit me at my weakness. Because I'd seen the signs with Ara and had ignored them because I'd thought I loved her, and in the end, I'd still refused to give her up, forcing his hand. Humiliation ate away, pinching my chest.

"This evening? She'll be in attendance then? Since the mating is... complete?" he asked, toying with his keys.

"She'll be there."

His grin was menacing. "Lovely."

Right.

He walked off.

And I stayed, planted in my seat, wondering if history truly was repeating itself, and if she wouldn't have been better off dying by Cassius's hands — dying in a blissful state — than living with someone who apparently had no capacity for love... or who, for some reason or another, was unlovable.

And that was the crux of the matter.

Regardless of what I'd done, my mate had never loved me back. Had never looked at me with the same adoration as I'd looked at her.

My love had destroyed her.

And in the end, I truly had no one to blame but myself, for being selfish enough to have hidden the truth from Cassius until it had been too late — selfish enough to have wanted to keep the child who hadn't even been mine.

Love, in all my experience, was just that — selfishness wrapped up in a pretty little bow.

I took one last drink of coffee and stood, just as a few giggling girls walked out of the coffee shop. They stopped. Their hearts, however, picked up speed as they glanced at me and blushed.

I didn't have time to placate them. Instead, I growled and stomped off in the other direction.

Stay alert.

Keep to the plan.

And above all — don't allow Genesis in. Because I wouldn't survive it a second time.

CHAPTER SIXTEEN

Genesis

I DIDN'T SEE ETHAN THE REST of the day. Stephanie tried to distract me with reality TV. It worked for a while, and then I'd gotten restless again. It wasn't that I was worried about him or anything. I just wanted to know that Cassius hadn't removed Ethan's head from his body. When I'd asked Alex about them fighting, he'd simply rolled his eyes and started talking about the Gathering that evening.

The women.

The lights.

The dancing.

But mostly the women.

It was time to go, and Ethan still wasn't there. I fidgeted with my dress, hoping it would please him and hating myself that it was even an issue. Why would I care? He'd rejected me over and over again only to offer me comfort and then reject me again. He made absolutely no sense, and in my current emotional state, I really desperately needed something to make sense.

Next to Stephanie, I felt like the ugly friend. The one you

took with you and forced your brother or cousin to dance with. As if on cue, Alex stepped forward and offered his arm.

It's not that I needed compliments — I'd lasted my entire life without them. I'd turned them away, knowing that if my number was ever called, I would never feel pretty again, because I'd be in the constant company of immortals.

Though I'd foolishly thought I'd be a type of teacher.

It was what I'd lived for, to either live to teach them or continue on with my boring life and find a career I was passionate about.

"Hey now," Alex whispered in my ear, "hold your head high. They'll smell your fear from a mile away."

"Fear isn't welcome," I repeated under my breath.

"Good girl." He patted my hand. "And you look gorgeous."

"Don't," I snapped. "Just... don't lie, please."

His eyebrows drew together; he opened his mouth but earned a slap on the shoulder from Mason.

I hadn't noticed his arrival. Mason was wearing dresspants and a shirt that left absolutely nothing to the imagination. Every muscle was outlined — it was hard not to stare. The man was huge. Had he not shown me compassion, I would be afraid of his size.

"She rides with me." He started prying my arm away from Alex.

Alex rolled his eyes. "Why not me?"

"She's safer with me, and those were Ethan's instructions. Check your phone."

Alex pulled out his iPhone. "Damn, how am I supposed to make an entrance without little human on my arm?"

"Name." Mason barked.

"Calling her human is my term of endearment, like sweetheart or babycakes."

"Call me babycakes, and I'll scratch your eyes out," my mouth fired off before I could stop it. Closing my eyes in embarrassment, I shook my head. "I'm sorry, I mean."

Alex barked out a laugh. "You're allowed to have opinions, babycakes."

I groaned.

"It's staying," he announced, "because it makes her turn red. Look."

He was pointing at my cheeks. I was sure they matched my dress. I'd just yelled at an immortal, threatened bodily harm, and he was laughing.

Mason removed Alex's hand from mine and took my arm. "Let's go, beautiful."

The attention, the compliments, the nicknames — they were too much. It was the opposite of what I'd expected, meaning, it was like being made fun of. Like I was naked for the class picture. It was embarrassing, being told I was beautiful when I knew, without a shadow of a doubt, that I paled in comparison to the ugliest of immortals.

"Did I say something wrong?" Mason asked once we were in his truck driving toward downtown. "You seem... upset."

My fingers slowly caressed the rich leather seats. I don't know what I expected him to drive, but a brand new GMC truck didn't really fit the image I'd had of werewolves.

"Um, no..." I lied. "It's nothing."

"You seem sad."

"Just... in shock, still."

"It will fade," Mason said in a calm voice. "It always does. My own mate, well, she..." His voice cracked. "She had a hard time at first."

"Was her number called?"

His eyes were black; it was hard to see where his pupils started and ended as he gazed at me then back at the road. "Yes."

"And you loved her?"

"Of course." He said it so quickly I didn't doubt him for one second. "With my entire life, my soul, my existence, I loved her."

"Loved."

"She simply…" His voice was hoarse. "She simply didn't wake up one morning. The evening before we'd been talking about children. The next morning she was cold."

"Mason…" I reached across the seat and grabbed his hand. "I'm so sorry."

He clenched my hand in his and brought it to his lips; his rough kiss across my knuckles warmed me from the inside out.

"It's not your fault."

"But…" My mind whirled. "I could change that? I could make it so that doesn't happen anymore?"

He was quiet for a while. "Possibly, but there's no way to know."

"So I live past a certain year, and what? We're home free?"

The truck pulled up to one of the hotels in downtown Seattle. It was newer, a boutique hotel right on the water. "Ethan wouldn't like me discussing such things with you. I'll allow him to explain."

"But—"

"That's all I'll say," he growled. "Now, let's go show you off to your mate."

The mate who hadn't even driven me to the Gathering?

The mate who hadn't spoken to me all day?

The same mate who'd looked like he wanted to shake me to death earlier that morning?

Great.

I choked back the fear at being in a room with possibly hundreds of immortals —in a room with Cassius himself — and followed Mason out of the truck.

He grabbed my hand again. I ducked against him, allowing his body to shield me.

He handed his keys to the valet, who eyed me up and down like I was a piece of candy.

Mason growled at the valet, who jolted out of his stare-down and ran toward the truck. "Idiots, all of the demons."

"Wh-what?"

"Demons." He shrugged. "Even hell won't take 'em, so they toil here for us until it's time for judgment."

"And then?"

"Hell welcomes them back with open arms."

I shivered.

"Are you cold?"

No, just completely freaked out. My studies had said nothing about demons. Nothing.

What other immortals hadn't I been told about?

I was almost afraid to ask.

Mason walked me through the doors of the hotel. Music sounded from somewhere in the lobby, or maybe it was the restaurant. The music grew louder as we walked toward it in silence.

When we stopped, it was in front of a black door.

Mason nodded to a tall man wearing head-to-toe black. He had an earpiece in his ear and examined the iPad in his hands. He turned the iPad toward Mason, who placed his hand on the screen.

It flashed green.

And the door opened.

I think, in my head I'd built the Gathering up to be something like I'd seen in horror movies — an orgy, blood-drinking, people in little to no clothing.

Instead... it was like I'd just walked onto a Hollywood movie set. Heads turned, both male and female, and they were flawless. My fingers dug into Mason's arm.

It wasn't fear.

More like awe. It had been hard enough to keep my jaw tight when I'd entered the throne room. This was a bazillion times worse.

Every woman in that room was perfectly proportioned —

tall, exotic, beautiful. There was no imperfection — at all.

The men, if I could call them that, since most of them were most likely immortal, were all pretty large in size and seemed more curious than anything. I noticed a few smiles in my direction.

A few sneers — from the women.

And in the far, far corner of the room, there were a group of people who looked like me, who looked normal, not like they belonged on the cover of a magazine.

"Humans," Mason whispered. "Over in the corner, most likely gossiping about their mates."

"What?"

On closer inspection, the humans looked... different. I couldn't really put my finger on it, but their skin was brighter than mine. Their eyes too. They just appeared extremely healthy.

There were both men and women, which I hadn't expected. Not that men's numbers had never been called. I just hadn't really thought about it much.

The room was decorated in blacks and silvers; long tables lined the walls, piled high with food and champagne.

The curious stares continued, so I clung to Mason like he was my lifeline; that was, until Alex came up beside me and offered a glass of champagne. "They stare because they're curious."

"They always stare at new humans?" I took a sip of the champagne, but it tasted off. I couldn't put my finger on it, but it seemed almost bitter on my tongue.

"No." Alex grinned. "Only you. Because of you who are, and well... you know... the fact that Ethan's your mate and Cassius started a pissing contest over you."

"Alex..." Mason rolled his eyes. "Stop."

"What?" Alex shrugged, and then his blue eyes brightened. "I think I see my conquest for the night."

A wave of heat washed over me; I didn't feel lust this time

or anything close to it, just heat. He winked, and then he was moving through the crowd to a tall, dark-haired lady with a black dress slinked around her body.

"Another siren?" I asked.

"Human." Mason nodded. "One of Alex's favorites."

"What?" I stopped him from walking. "Aren't all humans mated?"

"Er..." Mason scratched his head and looked around. "...Ethan really should explain that to you."

"Screw Ethan!" I stomped my foot. "He isn't here. You are."

The air around me crackled with warmth. Ethan.

"Hmm..." Ethan's smooth voice danced across the back of my neck. "Miss me that much, Genesis?"

Slowly, I turned and came face to face with sheer beauty. I couldn't look away even if I tried. His green eyes glowed against his smooth skin; long dark eyelashes fanned across his chiseled cheekbones. He was wearing all black — it should have looked ridiculous — a vampire in all black?

It didn't.

Look ridiculous, that was.

He looked edible.

I stepped away from Mason, not because I wanted to, but because my body couldn't help itself.

"Not every human mates... of course that's been the goal... but we do, at times, make exceptions for some. They want so desperately to be a part of our world that they're willing to do anything to be in it — even if it means they don't mate with an immortal. Getting screwed by one is enough."

"Harsh." Mason coughed.

"You've done your duty, Mason." Ethan looked over my shoulder. "Leave us."

Mason rolled his eyes and walked off.

"His duty?" I repeated.

"Take my arm," Ethan commanded.

"You've ignored me for an entire day, and you want me to take your arm?"

"You're my mate." He said it so simply, so matter-of-factly, that I wanted to punch him across his perfect mouth. "Take my arm, Genesis. You know you want to."

Every cell in my body screamed for me to take his arm and just be done with it, but I didn't want to give in, didn't want to give him the satisfaction.

"How was Cassius?" I asked, ignoring his outstretched arm and glancing away from him so I could gather myself.

"Cranky," Ethan hissed. "Like I'm about to be if you don't follow orders."

"Maybe if you said please," I whispered under my breath, "I'd be more likely to do your bidding."

"I could just kiss you into submission... bend you backward over the buffet table and have my way with you."

Lust surged through me. "I think that's the last thing you want to do."

His lips were suddenly grazing my ear. "Then you clearly don't know me very well."

"Whose fault is that?" My fingers clenched the champagne glass harder as I fought for control over my own body.

"Let's blame Alex." Ethan wrapped his muscled arm around my shoulders. "Now I'm sure in your studies you were told to respect immortals, that you were... *nothing* compared to us."

"Yes," I croaked.

"Good. So your first lesson is this... humans don't disrespect their mates, regardless of the circumstances. If I asked you to bend over and tie my shoe, I'd expect you to do it with a damn smile on your face."

"You're a jackass," I hissed, trying to pull away from him.

"I'm not actually asking you to tie my shoe, Genesis. I'm just telling you how it is. At a Gathering, there is a certain expectation. We talk, we show off our shiny treasures, and at the end of the night, we part ways, each of us comparing ourselves to one another. Every type of immortal is in attendance tonight. It would be good of you to stay by me, lest one of them trap you in a corner and try to take advantage."

"They'd do that? To you? Someone so old?"

His mouth pressed into a firm line. "I'm not that old."

"You are."

His arm tightened around my shoulder. "Great, then that makes you a child?"

"No, but—"

"They'd challenge me still, yes. And if Cassius approaches, try not to touch him, any part of him."

"What about breathing?" I tilted my head mockingly. "Am I allowed to do that?"

"Ethan!" Gushed a high pitched female voice from my right.

I turned and had the sudden urge to hide behind a potted plant, or maybe just Mason, wherever he'd gone. The woman was at least six feet tall, had long ebony hair, crystal green eyes, and a smile that seemed completely unreal.

"Where have you been?" She pushed me slightly out of the way, as if I didn't exist, and kissed him on both cheeks then pulled back.

"Busy," Ethan answered, tugging me yet again close to himself.

The woman's eyes squinted in my direction. "Oh…" She smirked. "Sorry. I didn't see you there."

Right.

Because I was ugly.

Nonexistent.

Worthless.

I tried to appear meek, but it seemed the longer I was in the immortal world the more anger issues I was developing. A week ago, I would have blushed and shrugged it off.

Now? I wanted to find a fork and stab her with it.

I clenched my fists together and offered a pathetic smile.

"She's the one then?" The woman kept talking. "I don't see it. I really don't. I heard Cassius is on a rampage."

"Cassius is always on a rampage." Ethan shrugged. "Delora, this is my mate, Genesis."

"Already?" Delora gasped. "Ethan, I thought—"

"It was great seeing you." Ethan dismissed her as if she were nothing but a tiny bug beneath his shoe. "I promised my love a dance though. Excuse us."

I fought the urge to snort. His love? Right.

Without asking me, Ethan set the champagne glass down on a nearby table and pulled me onto a small dance floor.

"She was lovely," I said once the music started.

A smile teased the corners of Ethan's mouth. "She's horrible, but at least you didn't throw your champagne in her face."

"I was tempted."

"Me too." His voice caressed my body. I tried to keep my distance from him, but he wasn't having it. Instead, he pulled me as close as physically possible so we were chest to chest. "I like your dress."

"It's red." *Lame. Someone, put me out of my misery.*

His warm chuckle had my knees shaking together. "Like blood."

"Yeah."

"About as damn tempting too."

I was desperate to hear him say it wasn't just the dress that was tempting, but me, even though I knew it was stupid, and I was just setting myself up to get hurt all over again.

"You look… nice."

Nice. He said I looked nice. Not pretty, not even cute, or beautiful, just nice. Like a dog.

Or a plant.

"Thanks." I swallowed the lump in my throat.

CHAPTER SEVENTEEN

Ethan

EVERY DAMN WOMAN IN THAT ROOM paled in comparison, and that was the truth. It was like fighting a war with myself — not telling her how I really felt, like dragging her away from the watchful eyes of people who'd do her harm and kissing her senseless then promising her forever.

It was instinctual.

Nothing more.

If I pushed her away, I wouldn't attach myself more emotionally — at least, that was what I told myself — then she'd gone and gotten cranky, which, frankly, was adorable.

She crossed her arms.

I half-expected her to stomp her foot or at least claw my eyes out. Damn, I would have been gone if she'd done any of those things.

She still had control.

I wondered if she noticed how her personality was slightly changing. Vampires weren't known for being calm and collected. Perhaps on the outside... but on the inside? Blood boiled; it always boiled. And I knew it was just a matter of time before she snapped.

Because my blood flowed through her veins, and if that didn't make me want to shout at the top of my lungs.

Her scent was covered up with perfume.

I didn't like it.

I sniffed her neck harder.

She flinched.

I licked.

And she froze in my arms.

I hadn't meant to actually lick her, or maybe I had, and I just hadn't fully thought through the ramifications of my actions.

"Sorry..." Since when did I apologize? "I was... curious."

"So you licked me?" Her body trembled in my arms.

I held her tighter. "Yeah." That's all I had.

The song was ending.

"What do I taste like?"

"Heaven," I said before I could lie. Being honest with her about her own taste was the least I could do, right?

But just admitting it out loud made me want more.

"What's heaven taste like?"

"Genesis." My mouth curved into a small smile at her swift intake of breath. Her heart picked up speed, like a horse getting ready to race. Her palms began to sweat against mine.

"Care to know how I taste?" I asked, dipping her low in my arms.

She blinked up at me. "Yes."

I almost dropped her on her ass. I'd been taunting her, teasing. I wasn't serious.

Slowly, I brought her back up to standing position. "Then take a bite."

"What?" she gasped.

"Just a small one..." I teased. "It's perfectly natural."

"But I'm a human."

Her cheeks were completely flushed; her heart beat faster

and faster. It was like a drug, listening to the physical effect I had on her body.

I raised her hand and twirled her twice, fast, and bit into my wrist on the third twirl. Three drops of blood met her lower lip.

She licked. Her eyes flashed green — my green.

And I lost complete control.

My mouth met hers in a frenzy; the perfect mixture of my blood and her taste was devastating to my senses.

What was worse?

Her hands had moved to my shoulders and were now fisting in my hair, tugging me closer, her body arching, trying to gain better access.

Her lips suddenly turned cold.

I pulled back and met Cassius's gaze across the room. He was smirking, the bastard.

Genesis shivered, her eyes confused. "What just happened?"

"I kissed you."

"Yeah, got that part." Her cheeks were still flushed. "But then it was cold... like before."

"A trick..." I turned her slowly.

Cassius nodded from his spot across the room.

Genesis leaned back against me, her knees buckling. "I want to go home now."

"You can't."

"What?" She turned in my arms, grabbing my jacket with her hands. "You mean we have to stay here all night?"

"Wait, what?" I shook my head. "Home as in... back to your mother?"

Her cheeks went bright red. "No, I mean... back to the house. Your house."

Home. She'd called my house her home. Male pride roared in my chest. Barely keeping it together, I nodded my head and pressed a kiss to her forehead.

"Yes, but first you must acknowledge Cassius."

"Why?" She dug her heels into the floor.

"Because he's as close to a king as we get, and every immortal, regardless of their feelings toward him, has to pay his respects."

Genesis reached for my hand, squeezing the life out of it. "But he won't hurt me, right?"

Pieces of her golden hair clung to her ruby red lipstick. I tugged them away and cupped her face. "He can't touch you — not with me here. I swear."

Nodding, she kept her tight grip on my hand as I led her through the crowd. The closer we got to Cassius the quieter it became. By now, it was no secret that I'd stolen Genesis from him — marked her, claimed her, and then had had the nerve to show up with her at the Gathering.

People knew our history.

But that didn't make what I'd done acceptable.

In fact, had I not been an Elder, I was pretty sure he would have ripped my heart from my chest and crushed it in his hand.

Cassius leaned against one of the tables, his arms crossed. He wore a smile that would make anyone — mortal or immortal — sell his soul for just one more.

I hated him in that moment, all over again, because I'd known an immortal once who'd been willing to do anything for one of Cassius's smiles or touches.

Feeling sick, I held Genesis tighter. Not her. Please not her. Cassius had taken everything from me. Would he take her too? Was she weak like Ara had been?

A lie.

It had all been a lie.

Just like my bond with Genesis was a lie.

I bit into my lip, drawing blood as Cassius's grin grew with each step we took toward him.

He was wearing a white button-up shirt, revealing half his

chest. I rolled my eyes. Dark Ones were vain, nice to look at, but they knew it.

At least vampires tried to appear humble.

Cassius knew he commanded the world and lived for that power.

"Genesis." Her name on his lips had me hissing aloud.

He grinned wider.

I imagined myself strangling him then removing his head from his body.

"Cassius," Genesis whispered.

The room was completely silent.

Cassius held out his hand.

Genesis looked at me, refusing to take his hand.

"Ah, he's taught you well." Cassius drew his hand back. "Apparently, your mate doubts your ability to stay true. If you really loved him... if the bond has truly worked... you'd be able to touch me and feel nothing. Did he tell you that?"

"Yes," she lied.

I could kiss her. I hadn't told her the truth — was afraid to — because of my own insecurities.

"I just don't want to disrespect Ethan."

Cassius's eyes narrowed in on Genesis. "Interesting."

Stephanie appeared by Cassius's side; he pulled her close to his body, his eyes going from blue to white then back again after releasing her. I didn't understand their special type of friendship, and a part of me didn't want to.

Sirens could become just as addicted to Dark Ones, and I hated to think that Stephanie had fallen into his trap like so many others before her.

Though her eyes stayed blue, and she didn't give off the normal chill a woman claimed would.

"Tell me, is the party to your liking, Genesis?" Cassius asked.

"It's beautiful." She wrapped her arm around my body, placing her head on my chest. "But Ethan promised me we'd spend some time alone tonight, so we're actually leaving."

Brave girl.

Cassius's eyebrows shot up.

"And does Ethan speak for himself these days, or do you do that for him?"

"Cassius," I warned. "Perhaps I like hearing her voice. I've been alive so long I've tired of hearing my own."

People around us laughed.

Genesis looked up at me adoringly.

So I did what any male would do in my position. I kissed her — hard. Our mouths fused together, our tongues tangled, and I forgot completely that I was in front of Cassius — or anyone. I lifted her against my body, my hands digging into her hair as she let out a little moan.

"Enough!" Cassius grunted out. "This isn't a brothel."

I released her, though it was hard, considering all I could focus on was the pulse of her heart through her swollen lips. I wanted to bite — again.

"Control yourself, Ethan," Cassius sneered. "Her blood will still be there when you get home. Then again, you're probably not going to be taking her blood, will you?"

Genesis hung her head.

"You know…" Cassius shrugged. "I wonder if it would be considered fair or loyal to your old mate? Taking a new one and destroying her as well?"

I released Genesis and pushed against Cassius's chest. "Take it back!"

He grinned and held up his hands. "My mistake."

Shaking my head, I stepped back and grabbed Genesis's hand. It killed me, absolutely killed me to bow my head to Cassius, to give him the respect he was due, when all I wanted to do was end his life. But I managed it, a slight bow.

He returned the sentiment.

And in a flash I was outside with Genesis.

When the demon threw me my keys, I almost threw them

back at his head, needing some sort of violent act to soothe me.

"Sorry." Genesis voice was weak, afraid. "I hope I didn't make things worse, I was just—"

"You," I turned and cupped her face, "did beautifully."

I kissed her again.

Because I could.

Because she calmed me.

Because I knew I couldn't claim her again in public, and I knew that once we got to the house, I'd have to leave her, lest I lose complete and utter control of myself.

When her arms snaked around my neck, I let out a pitiful growl and took a taste… just a few drops… directly from her tongue.

She gasped into my mouth, driving me into a frenzy to have her body closer.

Without thinking of her being as fragile as she was, I pushed her against the waiting car.

She let out a little grunt.

"Shit." I stepped back and pinched the bridge of my nose. "I'm sorry. I forget how fragile you are."

"Do I look broken?" Her eyes were shadowed, hazy, lustful. Damn, it was a beautiful look on her.

"No." I smirked. "You don't."

She reached for me.

I stepped back again, my breath coming out in gasps. "We should go."

The look on her face nearly brought me to my knees. I couldn't keep it up, kissing her and pushing her away, wanting her yet lying to myself about it.

"Okay." Again I was struck by how small her voice sounded.

I opened the door and ushered her in…

Then contemplated lying down in front of the car and asking the demon to hit the accelerator.

CHAPTER EIGHTEEN

Genesis

HE KISSED ME LIKE A MAN dying of thirst — and maybe he was, maybe it was my blood. Was it wrong to hope it was my smile? Maybe even my dress?

I played with the beautiful silk fabric, waiting for Ethan to acknowledge the kissing — or at least part of what Cassius had alluded to.

When the silence stretched the entire ride home, disappointment stabbed me in the chest.

We reached the house.

He pulled the car up to the massive gate; it opened.

Still nothing.

He turned off the car and reached for the door when I blurted, "Do you hate me?"

His hand froze on the car door; in fact, his entire body froze. My heart picked up speed. I knew he could hear it, but there was nothing I could do about the effect he had on me.

"No..." His voice was low, almost a growl. "I could never hate you."

"I'm sorry..." Tears stung the back of my eyes. "...for

whatever I did. I'm sorry you were forced to protect me when you didn't want to."

"You're apologizing?" His voice rose. "To me?"

My throat got tighter. "Yes."

He looked over his shoulder at me, his green eyes glowing in the darkness of the car. "You're tired."

"Yeah, but—

"We can talk tomorrow. I'll show you to your room."

So that was it.

My fingers clenched the silk dress tighter. I didn't trust myself to speak. The warmth I'd felt in his presence was long gone, replaced with nothingness.

He didn't even place his hand on my back as he led me into the dark house.

I walked mindlessly through the kitchen and up the stairs, not sure if I was even going in the right direction. A slight tap on my back to the left had me turning the corner at the end of the massive hallway.

Double doors.

Huge double doors.

They were at least twelve feet tall; two metal dragons twisted around the large doorknobs.

Ethan reached around me and opened them.

A roaring fireplace was the first thing I saw. It was see-through, and on the other side of the wall, I noted what looked like the bathroom. Extravagance dripped from every corner of the room — from the crystal chandelier suspended overhead to the sitting area with leather couches and fur throw pillows.

A matching fur rug lay in front of the fireplace.

The king-sized bed could fit at least five people. The down comforter was black and looked so plush that I was afraid I was going to get lost in it if I sunk too deep.

"Bathroom," Ethan whispered over my shoulder, "is to your right. I'll have Stephanie take you shopping later this week after you've grown accustomed to your new environment."

I nodded and turned to thank him, but he was already gone; the door shut in finality behind him.

Tears filled my eyes.

I wasn't sure why I was acting so emotional... other than being rejected. I'd been built for tougher situations, right? Hadn't I been prepared for the worst when I'd awakened — was it only twenty-four hours ago?

At least I wasn't dead.

There was that.

But I wasn't accepted, and I think a small part of me had hoped that maybe I would fit in this world better than my own.

I was smart enough to fit in.

I'd studied hard enough to make it a possibility.

But everything I'd studied had been a lie — or close enough.

My own mother hadn't given me the attention I'd craved — too afraid that if by chance my number was called, the separation would destroy me.

And now... I had the most beautiful man in the world kissing me — because he couldn't help himself.

Like a chocolate addict.

I was covered in his addiction; it flowed through my veins, but it wasn't me.

Slowly, I made my way into the bathroom. Expensive soaps lined one side of the tub. I started the hot water and began peeling my clothes away.

When the tub was full, I stepped in.

I'd just closed my eyes when I heard the doors open to the bedroom.

Ethan walked around the corner of the bathroom — like it was the most normal thing in the world — and held out a glass of wine.

I was too stunned to do anything but stare at the glass in

his hand; it shook slightly. "I figured this would help you relax."

With a gulp, I reached out, and took the wine glass. Our fingers grazed each other, causing a jolt of awareness to wash over my body. I imagined he felt it too, if the elongating of his fangs was any indication. Quickly, he looked away and walked out of the bathroom.

Slamming the door behind him.

AN HOUR LATER, AND I was in bed, too exhausted to sleep. The door to the room opened again.

I could make the outline of a body.

Then the person moved into the firelight.

"Ethan?"

His eyes started to glow in the darkness as he removed his shirt, followed by his pants, and every other article of clothing on his body.

Was he? Did he think something was going to happen?

I tensed beneath the covers.

"Relax..." His voice was both soothing and commanding. "...and try to sleep, Genesis."

With him. Naked. Next to me?

Right.

I was lucky I was still breathing. The man's body was made for sin. Muscle packed around his midsection so tightly it didn't look real. I blinked, thinking it was some sort of trick, because men really shouldn't be that good-looking.

Then again...

His eyes continued to glow.

He wasn't really a man, was he?

The bed dipped.

My erratic breathing increased. I closed my eyes and focused on calming down my own heart.

"I'm going to lose every ounce of control I have if your heart keeps beating that wildly whenever I take off my shirt." Ethan's voice held amusement, but I couldn't see his face, so I wasn't sure if he was smiling.

His warm hand touched my chest; his palm pressed against my skin. "Sleep, Genesis. Tonight... we sleep."

His words were like a drug, his hand was warm, and soon my entire body calmed down, sinking further and further into darkness.

"That's it..." His lips touched my ear. "Sleep."

My body was still fighting the sleep even though it sounded like a good idea.

Something warm trickled against my lips.

"Sleep," he commanded more forcefully this time.

My body immediately obeyed as I swallowed what I'd later discovered was his blood.

"So we meet again." Cassius grinned, holding out his hand.

I frowned. "Is this a dream?"

"I love dreams." He shoved his hands in his pockets. "So vivid, colorful — tell me, do you like the rainbow?" He pointed to the sky where the band of colors arched over us. We were on a boat on some sort of lake. "I created it just for you."

"Is this real?"

"As real as you allow it." His massive shoulders seemed to broaden as he inhaled deeply and motioned around him "Wonderful, isn't it? You share his bed, yet I can share your dreams."

"That seems incredibly invasive."

"Don't forget unfair." He winked.

"You're bad."

"Am I?" His deep laugh echoed through my body. "Or do you just wish I was bad in order to make yourself feel better about the choice that was forced upon you?"

"It was the only way."

He threw his head back and laughed. "Oh, believe me, it wasn't."

"You?" I bit down on my lip until it hurt. "Forgive me for not wanting to be taken by a Dark One... I've heard stories."

"Books lie." He shrugged. "Perhaps you would have survived me."

"Perhaps?" I repeated. "You're kidding, right?"

His eyes flashed. "Better."

I looked down. I was in a white bikini. I quickly tried to cover myself up; his laughter made me want to drown him. "May I have more clothing... please?"

His eyes flashed again, leaving me in a sarong. "Better?"

"No."

"Too bad." He leaned back on his elbows. "Ethan can't give you what I can."

"I'm not with Ethan because of what he can give me."

Cassius went still. "So they told you?"

"About the prophecy?"

He nodded.

"Yes."

"Did they tell you all of it?"

"Yes," I lied.

"I can smell the lie on your tongue." His eyes blazed white. "Never lie to me or any of my kind. It's infuriating and insulting to think you could get away with it in the first place."

Great, that meant he knew I'd been lying at the Gathering.

"Yes," his voice was smug, his smile matching it.

"Please... don't," I whispered.

"Don't?"

"Read me like that... I don't like it."

He studied me for a minute then gave a firm nod. "Fine. I won't pull the strings of your mind in an effort to give you exactly what you want before you even know you want it."

I clenched my teeth together. "What's the rest of the prophecy?"

"Why don't you ask your mate?"

"Because my mate is sleeping."

"Believe me..." Cassius laughed, the sound of it washed over me like he'd just stripped me naked. "The minute I invaded your dreams, he's been trying to wake you up. Sleep? He won't sleep until he knows you haven't touched me."

"If I touch you?"

Cassius's grin turned deadly. "Then I own you. Even in your dreams… you'd be mine regardless of the mating. Though, because you're bonded with Ethan, the desire to touch me lessens considerably, and there is that whole ridiculous issue with stealing you away from him since I can no longer smell you."

"Yet you can invade my thoughts? My dreams when I'm sleeping?"

"Only because I marked you first…" His eyes went white. A soft wind picked up, causing his black-as-night hair to blow across his face. "You think you've already made your choice — but you haven't, not yet."

"You or him." I nodded. "In the end, does it really matter?"

"Of course it does." Cassius said quickly. "Because there was once a human just like you… a human we thought was the one to fix everything and she failed. Care to know why?"

I didn't know how to answer. I wasn't sure if I could trust anything he said.

"She pretended… you see, Genesis. The prophecy specifically says a human will be called — she'll be the beginning of the end, she'll have golden hair…"

I touched my hair self-consciously.

"…eyes so beautiful an immortal could get lost in them."

I hung my head; I wasn't beautiful.

"You are breathtaking, more so than she could have ever hoped to be."

I looked up. "What happened?"

"She wanted too much," Cassius said in a sad voice. "And my hand was forced."

"I don't understand."

A soft rain started to fall. I held out my hands; the raindrops were blazing hot and turned to blood the minute they touched my *fingertips.*

"*His blood calls to you.*" Cassius nodded in understanding. "*Better return to him before he takes a bite.*"

"*But you didn't tell me—*"

I jolted awake to see Ethan hovering over me, his eyes completely black. "Tell me you didn't touch him. Tell me!" he roared.

I shook my head, my heart slamming against my chest. "I didn't touch him."

Ethan closed his eyes and swore. "I can't protect you in your dreams."

I reached for his face, shocked that he let me touch him now that the transition was over. "Then you'll have to trust me."

"Trust is earned."

"So let me try to earn it." I fought back angry tears.

He turned his head in my hand and kissed my palm. "I feel like I've already failed you. And that's the truth."

His breath was hot against my skin. I was afraid to move my hand, afraid it would shatter the moment. "Then stop failing."

"Not that simple," he whispered.

"Make it."

Black soulless eyes met mine. "Give me time."

"Do we have that? Time?"

He shuddered then leaned over me; his muscular body coming into contact with mine had me trembling with need. "I honestly hope so."

His lips grazed my neck.

I stopped breathing altogether.

"You taste like rain."

"I was on a lake."

"Dark Ones love water."

"Why?" I loved the feel of his lips against my neck as he talked.

"Because they love their own reflections."

I burst out laughing. It felt good.

Soon Ethan joined me and pulled my body on top of his. "Sleep, Genesis."

"No more dreams?"

"He can only invade once in a night."

"Oh... good." I yawned and stretched my arms above my head.

"Do that again, and I won't be held responsible for my own actions," he said in a husky voice.

"S-sorry."

"Don't be." He tugged my body against his.

It should have been uncomfortable, lying against his chest, but it was better than the bed.

"Now sleep."

CHAPTER NINETEEN

Ethan

"SO..." ALEX GRINNED OVER HIS CUP of coffee. "How was your evening?"

"It's too early," I growled. My body was still on fire. Sleep had been hell — or maybe heaven? Vampires still needed sleep, regardless of what silly books and movies said, and I'd gotten absolutely none.

Every breath she took I took with her, soaking her in, feeling her body move against mine. It was pure torture.

The human moaned.

She moaned! In her sleep! And clung to me like I was her lifeline. I hadn't felt that complete in a long time and didn't realize how hungry I was for that sort of affection until she freely gave it. Then again, she had been sleeping while I watched her.

"You're eyes are glowing," Alex mused.

"Why are you up? Didn't you take a woman home last night?" I desperately needed a subject change if I was going to make it through the rest of the morning with Genesis, teaching her, rubbing against her, smelling her. I nearly broke the mug in my hand just thinking about it.

"Kicked her out of bed after I was finished." Alex shrugged and examined his fingernails. "I bore easily."

"She wasn't entertaining enough?"

Alex let out a long snort. "It was only too easy. I asked her to strip — she stripped. I asked her to lie down on the bed — she lay down on the bed. Hell, I even asked the woman to purr—"

"Enough." I held up my hand.

"What?" Alex reached for his coffee and took another sip. "Boring. All of them. I need a challenge. Now Genesis—"

I hissed.

"Easy." He grinned. "I was only joking."

"Joke elsewhere."

Stephanie and Mason walked into the room, both of them wearing knowing smiles. Did everyone know of my hellish night?

"Ask him how he slept." Alex winked.

I threw a fork at his face. He moved his head out of the way, and the fork impaled itself into the wall.

"He's gotten quicker in his old age," Mason mused.

"It's all the women who throw things at him," Stephanie agreed. "Makes him quick."

"Oh please." Alex rolled his eyes. "They throw their bodies at me, would probably sell their souls if they could, and—" He coughed. "Hey, Genesis, you look well-rested. Happy. Content. Beautiful—"

"Alex." I stood, almost slicing my fingers through the table at his amused expression.

Genesis did look good.

Too good.

Gorgeous.

Flushed cheeks, red lips, gold hair.

I let out a groan, gaining everyone's attention, hers included. "Er, sorry... coffee got caught in my throat."

"You weren't drinking coffee," Alex pointed out.

"So..." Stephanie held out her hands to Genesis. "The jeans fit? I'm so glad. We'll go shopping later this week for more clothes, so you don't have to keep borrowing my stuff."

She looked perfect.

In jeans and a T-shirt.

My mouth watered the longer I stared.

Mason coughed.

I continued staring.

"Hungry?" Mason moved around the kitchen; pots started banging together. Genesis eyes locked onto mine.

I smiled.

She blushed harder.

One. Small. Lick.

I moved closer, only to be intercepted by Mason. "Let her at least eat before you... do anything."

I shook myself out of my stupor and gave a firm nod. "Food, right. Eggs?"

Genesis flashed me a smile then turned her attention to Mason. "Eggs would be great, but I can cook."

"Nope." Mason shook his head fiercely. "A woman's place is not the kitchen."

"Really?" Genesis looked dumbfounded.

"Course not," Alex joined in cheerfully. "It's the bedroom."

I groaned.

Genesis let out a small laugh and shook her head. At least she could pick up on when they were joking and didn't stomp back up the stairs in frustration at our backward ways.

Mason cooked while Alex stole every single ounce of Genesis's attention. Stephanie shared a pitiful look with me. Right, something's wrong in the world when a female siren feels sorry for a vampire.

I cleared my throat.

Genesis looked up.

"Would you like to take a tour of the house while Mason finishes up?"

"Sure."

I held out my hand.

"Careful." Alex stood and placed his hands on her shoulders. "If he gets you alone, you may not get breakfast..."

"Hilarious." I rolled my eyes.

"If he's hungry, I don't mind feeding him." Genesis's smoldering gaze met mine.

I swayed a bit on my feet as my fangs dug into my lower lip. I could actually feel my blood soar from my chest out to my fingertips as I anticipated her taste. Hell, I was in deep. My hands started to shake.

"Careful with your promises, human." Alex's lips curved into a smile. "He may just take you up on it."

Genesis took my hand, ignoring Alex, thank God, and squeezed.

We made it as far as the hallway.

I'd like to think I had enough self-control to make it further than that. I was old, controlled — but I'd never had her before.

And she made all the difference.

My fingers dug into the skin on her wrist as I tried to think of a sentence — any sentence — that would make sense, that I could say.

All I had was "Look, a hallway."

It was Genesis, the meek, brave little human, who stopped, lifted her head and said, "I don't mind."

Three words.

I don't mind.

Three words. They weren't romantic. They held no lust, no desire, nothing — but to me it was trust. It was her trying.

So I gently pushed her against the wall and took her mouth with all the slowness she deserved.

Blood soared through her veins.

I'd only taken small amounts, enough to satisfy, enough to taste, enough to complete the bond.

I'd only planned on taking another few drops.

But she turned her head, causing my fangs to graze down her neck.

Blood dripped.

So I licked, savoring the feel of her warmth on my tongue.

And when I accidentally grazed her again...

I bit.

CHAPTER TWENTY

Genesis

THE MINUTE HE BIT DOWN — I KNEW-I'd just done something I couldn't undo... experienced something I would never, in all my days, be able to forget.

He said I'd know when he bit.

What he'd meant was I'd know when he finally gave into his instincts. It wasn't fast, like I'd expected, where he greedily sucked, pulled from my life source until I was drained.

Instead, the minute his teeth slid into my neck...

The world stopped.

Time stopped.

I closed my eyes, only to open them again and watch the world go by me in slow motion. Dust flicked in front of my face. The clock on the far side of the hallway moved... slower. Everything was slowed, even my heartbeat, and for those brief seconds or maybe even minutes...

I felt every single part of him.

Every stretch of muscle.

Every breath.

His pleasure was mine. It was almost hard to breathe

because my senses were so overwhelmed with not only him, but with the world around me. The world I'd always known to be normal... was anything but normal.

The color of the wall had been blue.

Now it was electric blue.

Even Ethan's skin looked different, almost transparent as he clung to my body, his fingers digging into my flesh.

It was indescribable, and I was failing at trying to soak everything in.

His tongue swirled across my neck, and then I felt him draw a little bit more; this time the feeling changed, and suddenly all I could smell was burnt sugar — like Christmas, only better.

My body felt heavy; it pulsed in perfect cadence with him.

Ethan sighed against my neck, and the world returned to normal bland colors. The clock finally made it to the next minute.

And I had to fight to keep myself from crying out for him to keep going.

"I'm sorry." His voice was so low, so hoarse it was almost hard to understand his words. "I — you—" He cursed and pulled back.

His eyes were so green that I looked away. I had to because I was afraid if I kept staring, they would somehow burn my irises, blinding me.

"Don't be," I whispered. "I offered. Besides, you pulled me from my dream last night. It was the least I could do, right?"

"You have no idea," his lips lingered in front of mine, grazing my mouth with each word he spoke, "how good you feel — how wonderful you taste."

I leaned forward; the temptation to kiss him was too much.

A throat cleared. "Uh, do you still want eggs?"

I pushed against Ethan's chest, taking a step back, and

glanced at Mason. His eyes betrayed nothing, so I wasn't sure if he'd seen us, or if he'd just assumed I'd been offering up myself as Ethan's breakfast.

"Yes," Ethan answered for me. "She's lacking protein."

"Huh?" I asked, dumbfounded. "How would you know...?"

He smirked.

"How's my iron?"

"Perfectly balanced."

We shared a smile. It felt good to talk to him like he didn't hate me, yet I still felt like I had no choice but to keep my guard up. It was a tie between wanting to open up to him, yet knowing that if I did and he rejected me again, I'd have no one to blame but myself.

I needed to remember he was still an immortal.

School really hadn't prepared me for what I was up against.

"Eat," Ethan urged. "I'll wait for you in the study. We can go over your horrible education after Mason's convinced you've eaten enough."

Mason held up the pan of eggs again in his hand.

Ethan kissed my head and left, leaving me and Mason alone in the hallway.

"So..." Mason moved out of the way so I could step by him. "Good morning so far?"

I fought to hide my grin. "The best."

"Wait until you eat my eggs."

"You mean it gets better?" I joked, elbowing him in the side.

"Yes, but be warned, I made the whole carton on account I'm used to cooking for more than one person. You'll insult me if you don't eat. Besides, according to your mate, you're lacking in protein."

I rolled my eyes and sat at the table while Mason served me an ungodly amount of eggs.

Both Stephanie and Alex were nowhere to be found.

I shoveled some eggs into my mouth and fought back a moan. The man could cook. They might tease him about eating berries and pinecones, but his eggs were fluffy. "So what do you guys do during the day?"

"As opposed to during the night?" Mason laughed. "Tell me, are you under the impression I go outside and howl at the moon when night falls?"

I felt my cheeks heat.

He barked out a laugh. "I may sit in on your studies this afternoon just so I can watch you blush the entire time."

I poked a few more eggs. "So?"

"The four of us are Immortal Elders, not only do we each have business holdings all over the world — ones we're still very much involved in — but we keep the peace."

I frowned. "Like the police?"

"Sort of." Mason shrugged. "I guess, in a way, I'm pack leader. I check in on the different families of werewolves in the Greater Seattle area and keep in constant communication with them. Some of the families like to live outside of the city and, naturally, outside of the country, so I get reports on them on a daily basis."

"Alex and Stephanie? What about them?"

"Sirens," Mason leaned back in his chair and lifted a mug of coffee to his lips, "tend to focus on play more than work."

"Meaning?"

"Curious little thing, aren't you?"

"Well..." I put down my fork. "I'm curious because, to be honest, when I was in school, I was taught you guys kept to yourselves. Nothing ever mentioned jobs or hobbies. I guess I assumed you just sat around and thought about your own immortality."

"How boring..." Mason's eyebrows lifted. "To sit around and only think about yourself. Sounds more like a Dark One than a werewolf."

"Is that what they do?"

"I'll let Ethan explain exactly what Dark Ones do, other than rule with an iron fist and petition archangels."

My ears perked up. "Real archangels?"

"No, fake ones… we just like the name because it sounds cool." He smirked. "Yes, real ones."

"You've seen them?"

"Once, a very long, long time ago. As long as we keep the peace between all species, they don't interfere. They have no reason to."

"And if war breaks out?"

Mason glanced over my shoulder, his eyes drawn to the hallway. "Ethan's irritated with me for keeping you so long. Two more bites then go back down the hall, first door on your left."

"But—"

"Two bites." Mason held up two fingers. "And then you get to go to school with a vampire."

I felt myself blush again because all I could think about was Ethan, in all his sexiness, trying to teach me something — anything — in that deep seductive voice of his. Yeah, it was going to be a really long day.

CHAPTER TWENTY-ONE

Ethan

I PACED IN THE STUDY LIKE someone who'd just drunk an entire pot of coffee and needed to work it out of his system.

All I tasted was her.

Her blood was still on my tongue — on my lips — and her memories, the ones that came with her blood — the ones that came at the price of me sharing my own — were so horrific I'd checked my watch at least five times to see if I'd make it across town and back without her knowing.

I wanted to murder her mother.

And the rest of the humans she'd been studying with.

Yes, secrecy was necessary, but to force the humans to think so little about themselves — especially Genesis — was criminal.

She was nearing. I could smell her.

Two footsteps and she'd be in the room.

And I'd probably lose my mind with the madness that always came with her scent.

"Nice study." Her voice was husky, dripping with seduction without even trying.

I broke the pencil in my hand and dropped it to the ground, turning on my heel, knowing that just staring at her would cause my heart to pound.

"Thank you." I managed the words between my lips, but they sounded more like a hiss — or possibly a choked whisper.

She pointed at one of the chairs. "Are we sitting?"

The damn chair taunted me. What I wouldn't do to have a king-sized bed in that room I could toss her onto.

I coughed into my hand. "Yes, the chair is fine."

Genesis tucked her golden hair behind her ears and sat, folding her arms across her chest. "So, school's in session?"

And you've been a very bad, bad, girl.

I groaned and turned back around, focusing on the dusty textbooks lining the walls. "Yes... why don't we start with what you know. Or at least what you've been learning up until now."

She took a deep breath.

I waited.

Still not turning back to face her because I was having a hell of a time keeping my body under control.

"I'm ugly."

Not what I expected.

"What?" I hissed, nearly knocking over the table in front of me to get to her. "What did you say?"

Her face paled. "The first phrase I remember as a child."

"Explain." Murder was definitely going to be on the agenda. Exquisite, painful, spectacular, satisfying murder.

Experiencing her memories of indoctrination by humans who were supposed to love her, provide for her, protect her, was one thing. But hearing the testament of the ugliness she was forced to endure—it was hell. It was heartbreaking, to still have her taste on my lips — to know the purity of her soul — and hear the firsthand account of a mother who basically spat in her face.

"I think most normal children imagine their first Christmas or their first birthday. All I can remember from my childhood is my mom telling me that I was ugly. She even wrote it on a piece of paper and put it on the bathroom mirror so I wouldn't become vain."

"Why would she do that?"

"It may sound cruel." Genesis nibbled her lower lip as tears filled her eyes. "But it's what we've been taught all our lives. We'll never live up to immortal standards, never be loveable, never be beautiful. We're mere objects. We study as hard as we can so that if our number is called, we can do a good job and bring honor to our families. My family has a sort of black mark on it for reasons my mother never told me. I never expected my number to be called, but in case it was, that's the only phrase she kept repeating to me. *You are nothing. You are ugly.*'"

"It's a lie," I whispered fiercely, taking her chin in my hands so she couldn't look away. "It's an absolute falsehood. You aren't ugly."

"It's okay if I am." Genesis's eyes were glassy with tears. "I mean, compared to immortals I'm—"

"Perfect," I finished for her. "And if I ever hear you say that about yourself again, you'll be punished."

"Punished?"

I released her chin. "Yes… I'll force you to eat pinecones instead of Mason's eggs."

She let out a laugh.

"You're beautiful, Genesis." I swallowed, placing my hands on the table in front of her. "Immortals would fight wars over you, and not just your face or your hair or the way your smile penetrates to someone's very soul — but because you're good."

"You don't know that. I could be a horrible person…"

"Your blood would taste bitter," I said honestly, "because the emotional manifests into the physical. Your blood would be repugnant to me, and other immortals would shy away from you because the last thing any immortal wants is to mate with a human who is pure evil."

"Oh..." Her breathing picked up speed. "They didn't teach us that."

"They wouldn't. It's a secret." I winked.

Her smile brightened considerably. "Thank you... for saying that. But it's hard to believe you after everything I've already seen and the way I seem to repel you and—"

I burst out laughing. "Oh, Genesis, if only you did repel me, things would be so much easier."

Her eyebrows furrowed together; I could read the frustration on her face.

"What else?" I sat down on the table in front of her. "What did they teach you?"

"They taught us that you scorned technology, that you didn't have time to teach your children what was necessary to survive, so as humans, it would be our job to educate your children as well as the families we were placed with."

"A glorified nanny."

"Yes." She nodded. "Exactly. And if we served the family well, then word would spread and more immortals would want me or my bloodline specifically."

"I wonder..." I tapped my chin. "Why they would lie?"

"Maybe because telling us our only job as a human was to become a mate to an immortal would terrify some people?"

"Possibly..." My mind reeled. None of it made sense. Sure, we'd kept our secrets over the years to protect ourselves, to protect the humans from getting greedy. "A hundred years ago, the schools taught respect for immortals and gave you knowledge about our world, about your place in it, about the balance. Why would they suddenly change that?"

Genesis shrugged. "If I had to guess, it may be because humans started dying. You said so yourself."

"There is that." I gritted my teeth together, suddenly

worried that I wasn't doing enough to nourish her, to take care of her. It was my job, damn it!

"Ethan?" She licked her lips and leaned forward. "Your eyes are turning black again."

"Yes, they do that."

"Why?"

"Because they can."

"Seriously?"

I smiled. "No, because sometimes I can't control myself. They lose color when I'm feeling something extreme. The green simply fades into black. A lack of color doesn't mean I'm soulless or anything ridiculous. It just means the vampire blood has spread to other parts of my body, readying me for a fight."

"Hmm…"

"Your eyes turn green too, you know."

"What?" Her eyes widened. "What do you mean?"

"I've shared blood with you. When you're feeling something extreme, your eyes will turn green like mine. They match your mate's. You'll also notice that you don't need as much sleep as usual. Your skin will become softer. Think of it as having a very nice beauty regimen." I laughed at her excited expression. "You're welcome?"

"Wow."

"Not that you need it," I added quickly. "The last thing you need is to offer more temptation for me and my kind."

She didn't say anything.

"I'm curious to learn more about you," I said honestly. "But I don't want to keep you cooped up in the study all day. You don't seem like the type who enjoys studying."

She sighed. "What gave me away?"

"Your emotions easily betray you — and if they didn't, your blood surely would."

Red stained her cheeks, causing all of my blood to once again whoosh from my face to my lower extremities—only this time I wasn't bracing for a fight, but for a few hours tangled in bed with her.

"Why don't I take you to that bookstore we told you about? You can meet Drystan and see if it's something that you'd enjoy doing while I work."

"You work?"

"I'd like to think so."

"Like Mason?"

"Like Mason. Unlike Stephanie and Alex, however." I held out my hand. "I'll show you after the bookstore. Would you like that?"

"Yeah." She took my hand then squinted down at it.

"Something wrong?"

"I'm just trying to figure out what a vampire does for a job."

I barked out a laugh and wrapped my arm around her shoulders. "Yes, well, I think I may keep you in suspense until later."

She leaned into me.

I inhaled her scent, and my body shuddered with awareness.

It was horrible knowing that my reaction to her was so strong, yet she had no idea the war that raged inside of me, the desire I had to tell her everything, to cut myself open and show her my pain, my shame, and ask her to take it all away.

I was balancing with my life — possibly hers.

And yet, I couldn't find myself to regret anything.

Not anymore.

Not after talking with her.

Not after truly tasting her.

"Hungry again?" she asked.

"What?"

"You were licking me."

"Uh…" Damn it, I really needed to stay focused. I moved away from her, enough to evade the temptation of her neck.

"Sorry."

She glanced up at me through hooded eyes. "It's okay."

I growled.

She bit her lower lip.

And again, we were in the damn hallway. What was it about the hallway that destroyed every shred of sense I possessed?

"Ethan?" Mason called from the kitchen. "You going out?"

"Yeah...." I called, never taking my eyes from Genesis. "The bookstore."

"Get me berries!" he yelled. "We're out."

I shook my head, the spell broken. "Eat meat, for God's sakes, wolf."

"Berries," he repeated.

Genesis laughed softly.

"Damn berries." I led her to the door. "Shall we?"

"Should we ask him if he needs pinecones too?"

A pinecone flew by my head. "Clearly, he still has some left if he's using them as ammo."

CHAPTER TWENTY-TWO

Genesis

"I'VE BEEN HERE BEFORE," I BLURTED when Ethan pulled up to a downtown book shop around fifteen minutes from his house. It was one of my favorites. It had the best scones in the world, and the coffee was well-known in the area. "It's called Wolf's."

"Funny, right?" Ethan smirked.

I rolled my eyes and got out of the car. Did that mean I'd met the owner before? The bookstore wasn't huge like a Barnes and Noble, but it was big enough that it had two levels and multiple employees.

The bell on the door chimed as Ethan opened it and ushered me in. The smell of books was so familiar my knees almost gave way.

"Ethan." A man who looked like he was around my age smiled in our direction and made his way toward us. He seemed younger than Mason even; he had the same shaggy hair and really dark brown eyes — almost black. "So this is... Genesis."

"Hi." I waved awkwardly, unsure of how I was supposed to address him since, technically, nobody knew what he was.

He grinned. "You're cute."

Ethan growled.

"I meant it in an innocent way." Drystan held up his hands. "Easy..." He turned his attention back to me. "You've got the job."

"Just like that?"

"Just like that."

"But what if I'm horrible at it?" I blurted.

Drystan laughed. "If an Elder vouches for you — well, it's as good as done. Now, why don't I go over the schedule with you while Ethan makes himself scarce. Are you okay with starting work tomorrow? I had to fire someone yesterday for stealing, so I'm a bit shorthanded."

"Sure."

I was about to follow him when Ethan tugged me back and whispered in my ear, "Be careful."

A cold chill settled over me. I wasn't sure why I needed to be careful, considering he was going to be leaving me alone with this guy for hours on end, but I decided to listen to him regardless.

"Schedule..." Drystan moved toward a workstation located in the middle of the store. "...is always kept on the computer. And we do all our sales through Square, so we don't really have a typical cash register. Are you familiar with it?"

Technology. Yes. I was the one who was supposed to be teaching them — at least at one point. I nodded.

"Good." He clapped his hands together. "We get new books every Tuesday. You'll have to sign for them, and if we aren't busy, you're free to stock the shelves." He pointed behind him. "Books that are left out need to be reshelved at the end of the day and, luckily, you don't have to make coffee or scones. My wife does all that."

"Wife?"

He grinned. "We work together. It's a mate thing."

"Do all mates work together?"

His eyes darted behind me as if looking for Ethan. "Well, it's different for each of us."

"Oh."

"I'll pay you fifteen an hour. Though it's not like you need it, considering who you're with."

I blushed. I didn't like the idea of owing Ethan anything; somehow it felt wrong. I didn't deserve it, didn't earn it, and regardless of how well things were going that day, I had no idea if one minute he was going to get tired of me, and I'd need money for some reason.

"Great." I found myself shaking his hand, excited that I wouldn't be stuck at the house and would be able to actually contribute to society.

Drystan squeezed my hand, then flinched and jerked it back, like I'd hurt him.

"Is everything okay?" Ethan asked, approaching us.

Drystan shared a look with him. "Ethan, a moment?"

Ethan's smile was forced. "Sure. Genesis, why don't you pick out some books?"

I nodded and watched them walk off.

Had I done something to offend the werewolf? Everything had seemed fine until I'd touched him.

He'd flinched.

Why would he flinch?

I started mindlessly walking the aisles of books, when I heard Ethan's growl.

Slowly, I moved closer until I could hear his voice.

"I can't protect her if he comes." Drystan's voice was frantic. "I have a family, Ethan."

"He won't."

"He could bring them down on me and my family. You know he could, and I don't know how much time I have left with her — before she dies like the others. I don't want to spend that time worrying that a Dark One's going to kill me."

Ethan sighed heavily. "Trust me."

"I do. You know I do. It's her I don't trust."

What? That made no sense! I was a mere human!

"She's trustworthy," Ethan barked. "You dare insult my mate?"

"You dare bring in a marked one?"

"We've bonded — it's done."

"But it's not," Drystan argued. "Not unless she fully gives herself to you — you know that."

"She will."

Drystan swore. "How long do you have?"

Ethan's breathing picked up. "We have time."

"How much?"

"This is ridiculous. I'm an Elder."

"Ethan—"

"She's already chosen."

"No." Drystan's voice was distant. "She hasn't. Ice still flows through her veins. She may have said the words, but she isn't there, not yet, and until she is, he will continue to come for her."

I was listening so intently that I almost let out a yelp when Ethan called for me.

I grabbed the first two books I saw and ran around the corner to find him. He didn't seem on edge, but I knew he was. I could feel the distance building around his body again.

"What books did you choose?"

I looked down at the books in my hands and almost choked. "Um, you know what? I don't need any books today."

He rolled his eyes. "Give me the books, Genesis."

"I think I've changed my mind. I'm just going to go—"

He snatched them out of my hands and looked down. I knew the exact moment he'd read the titles.

Because he started shaking.

His eyes flashed black then green then black again as he looked at me, his fangs elongating.

I took a step back.

Drystan pretended to ignore us.

And my heart picked up speed as Ethan's gaze devoured me.

"We'll take these." He set them on the table, his smile indulgent. "It seems my human likes to... study."

Drystan gave nothing away as he scanned the books, took Ethan's change, and handed him the bag.

"See you tomorrow, Genesis."

I waved with my free hand while Ethan placed a death grip on my other. Yeah, things were about to get embarrassing really fast.

The minute we were outside, he pushed me into the car.

The silence was thick. Tense.

"So," Ethan spoke in a gravelly voice, "'Three Hundred and Sixty-five Positions for Three Hundred and Sixty-Five Days.'"

My body flamed.

"And what was the other?" He scratched his head. "'Kama Sutra for the Advanced'?"

I banged my head against the car's window. "In my defense, I was distracted."

"Mmm, care to share what had you so distracted?"

"No."

"I feel very much distracted," Ethan mused. "In fact, I may need you to distract me from the distractions."

My heart picked up speed. "Oh?"

"Yes."

He said it like a mere whisper, but I felt it in my chest. I felt the yes everywhere. I gripped the leather seat with my hands to keep from reaching for him.

"Work," I blurted. "You said you'd show me what you do."

"I'm not thinking about work right now."

I trembled.

"Care to know my fixation?"

I turned, slowly making eye contact with him. "Books?"

"Genesis." He said my name like a vow.

I reached for him at the same time he reached for me. Our mouths collided; warmth spread from my chest down to my toes as he lifted me from my seat.

And then a sudden chill filled the air.

Abruptly, he let me go and cursed. "He's close. Let's go."

Freaked out, I buckled my seatbelt and almost hit my head on the dash as Ethan peeled out of the parking spot. When I glanced at the rearview mirror, it was to see Cassius standing on the curb, blowing an ice-filled kiss in my direction.

"FISH," I REPEATED IN disbelief. "That's your job?"

"What?" Ethan shrugged.

After our *almost*-run-in with Cassius, Ethan had decided it was best to confuse the Dark One and get my scent all over Seattle.

We'd gone to at least three bakeries, two Starbucks, bought flowers, berries, and finally ended up by the pier.

The building said *Immortal Industries.*

Talk about blatant.

"You ship fish?" I still couldn't believe it.

"Worldwide." Ethan grinned. "Disappointed?"

"The name needs work."

"Yes, well, I decided that sometimes the best way to hide is to do the opposite of hiding." He frowned. "You're cold?"

I shivered. "A bit."

He wrapped his arms around me. "It's Cassius."

"You lied to me."

His breathing slowed. "Eavesdropping is frowned upon — always."

"What aren't you telling me?"

"A lot."

"At least you're honest about that much."

Ethan went very still. My back was to him; his arms wrapped around my body, warming me from the inside out. "I'd have to show you — talking about it is too difficult."

"Is it scary?"

"No." His lips touched my neck. "Just very sad, embarrassing, a lot of other unfortunate emotions."

"Show me."

"Not here."

"Yes, here." I turned in his arms. "Eventually, you're going to need my help, right? You can't just keep information from me then expect the bond — or whatever we have — to make up for everything else. We're at least friends, right?"

His eyes widened. "Yes."

"And friends share."

"They do."

"And you drink from me."

"Shhh..." He pulled me closer. "Yes."

"So, you owe me this. Honesty, you owe me."

"You raised your voice." He sounded amused.

"Yeah, well... you make me angry."

Another heavy sigh. "If I show you, you may leave me."

"I'd have a choice?"

"We always have a choice, Genesis."

"So trust me to stay."

He was still again; his heartbeat slowed — I could feel it like it was my own. Finally, he answered with a brisk, "Alright."

We walked in silence back to the car.

"It's safer at the house," he whispered. His gaze no longer had light in it; it was like the conversation sucked all the energy, all the spark from his body, leaving him haunted.

When we walked hand in hand through the door, Mason was waiting. Ethan chucked the berries at Mason's head and dragged me down the hall and up the stairs.

Once we were blanketed in the silence of the bedroom, the doors locked behind us, Ethan turned, his eyes black, his fangs elongated. "Promise me to wait ten minutes."

"What?"

"Ten minutes. When you wake up, wait ten minutes before you decide to leave or stay. At least give me that."

"Okay..." I swallowed the lump in my throat. His heart was breaking, I could feel it, and I had no idea why. "Ten minutes."

His teeth ripped into his wrist, and then that same wrist was pressed against my mouth. "Try to understand..." His last words before sleep overcame me.

Before a dream appeared in front of my eyes.

Before I came face to face with the most beautiful woman in the world. The same one from Ethan's dreams when the transition had occurred.

Her eyes danced with life.

Ethan adored her.

I adored her.

She danced around him.

He laughed and tugged her across his body. "I love you."

"I love you too, silly." She drank from him freely, yet she was human. She had fangs — just like Ethan. But I knew she was human. I could feel it.

"Make me immortal." She pouted, bracing herself over his body. "It's time already."

"After our child is born, it will happen. You know this."

"I'm tired of waiting."

Her pouting was getting on my nerves. Rage poured through me as she dragged her fingernails down his chest. That was my chest; those lips were my lips.

I clenched my fists at my sides and kept watching.

More scenes of them laughing, playing.

I tried to look away, but it was impossible.

Cassius appeared. I flinched, thinking it was a trick, but he was part of the dream.

"And how is my favorite girl?" He kissed her palm.

"Upset." She put her hands on her hips. "He refuses to make me immortal."

"Is that what you want? Your greatest desire?"

She nodded.

"Above Ethan, even? Your own mate?"

"He may be my mate..." Her hands trailed down Cassius's chest. "...but we both know I have a wide range of tastes."

"If you don't truly love him, the change will kill you." Cassius pushed her hand away. "You know this."

"I do love him!" She twirled around. "I love everything about this life. Is it so wrong to want more?"

"Sometimes..." Cassius's face fell. "...it really is."

The scene changed.

Cassius was walking with Ethan. "She's going mad."

"I know."

"It's the power — your power's drugging her, Ethan. You must let her go."

"No!" Ethan roared, pushing at Cassius. "I could no more cut out my own heart, you know that!"

"It's you or her," Cassius said.

"She's pregnant."

Cassius cursed and looked away. "Is it yours?"

"How dare you!" Ethan roared. "Of course it is!"

"And you know this for a fact? Because your mate is true?"

"I'd know if she weren't. I'd taste it in her blood."

"Unless you were too blinded by your own feelings... friend." Cassius shook his head again. "If the madness overtakes her, if you're wrong, you'll have to kill her yourself."

"I'm not wrong."

"So arrogant."

"Are we done here?"

I blinked away the tears. How could Cassius ask that of Ethan? I felt the love he had for her; it was powerful, like a star exploding in the sky.

"A daughter!" Ethan laughed and held up his son. "Ara! You've given me a daughter!"

She nodded.

The scene from the dream replayed, only slightly different than what I'd watched before.

Cassius entered the room.

Ara, Ethan's mate, looked away from both of them.

"I told you what would happen," Cassius said. "I warned you." He reached for the child.

"No!" Ethan screamed. "Don't. Cassius if you do this—"

"It's already been done." Cassius turned and pointed his hand at Ara. "Is this the daughter of a vampire?"

She trembled beneath the blankets then burst out laughing. "No, no, you know whose daughter she is."

Ethan paled. "Ara? My love?"

"He promised me immortality." Ara pointed at Cassius. "So give it! I birthed a daughter! The daughter of a Dark One! I will be queen!"

Her laughter hit a point where I needed to cover my ears.

"Cassius?" Ethan whispered. "Tell me you did not do this. Tell me, brother, that you did not—"

"She was tested. She failed," Cassius said simply, grabbing the child. "Now finish it."

"Cassius!" Ethan roared.

Ara continued to laugh. "I'm going to be queen. Finally, Ethan. I'm sorry I didn't tell you, but I was afraid you'd be angry. You know I love you, yes?"

Ethan's eyes turned black; the entire room shook.

"You bitch!" He clenched his fists so hard blood began trickling from his palms. And then, in an instant, he was on top of her.

One bite.

She struggled for two seconds.

Before I felt her life-force leave the room.

"It's done." Ethan swore, falling to his knees, blood dripping down his face.

"She would have died regardless," Cassius answered.

"My daughter."

"She's not your daughter, brother."

Ethan's eyes flashed. *"Give me my child!"*

"One day," Cassius started to fade into the darkness, *"you'll thank me."*

"One day... I will kill you."

Cassius disappeared from the room with the newborn, his voice a mere whisper. *"You can't."*

I woke up gasping for air.

I was lying in bed. Ethan was a statue next to me.

"Y-you killed her!"

Tears streamed down my face. I hated him. Hated us. I couldn't explain it, but the anger he'd felt — I felt; the shame — it was mine. I tasted revenge on my tongue. I wanted to scratch his eyes out, yet scratch my own out because it was like I was the one who had committed murder.

The darkness consumed me.

"Ten minutes," Ethan whispered.

"No."

"You promised."

He reached for my hand.

When I didn't take it, he straddled me and pinned my arms to the mattress. "Ten minutes. You promised. In ten minutes, I'll release you. Not a second sooner."

"Get. Off."

"He can still take you from me — like he took her."

"She chose herself, not him."

Ethan nodded sadly. "Yes."

I struggled against him, but he was too strong.

"Ten minutes, Genesis."

CHAPTER TWENTY-THREE

Ethan

HER EYES WERE GREEN.

Just like mine.

I felt her emotions like they were my own — relived the entire thing as if I was killing Ara all over again.

She'd done the unthinkable. She'd not only lied to her mate but cheated on him and produced a child with that lie. I knew Genesis wouldn't understand. But I also knew trying to get her to understand while she was still trembling from shock wouldn't do any good.

"You didn't have to kill her." Genesis's voice was hollow, her eyes still blazing green.

"I did." I touched my forehead to hers. "Because if I didn't, Cassius would have."

"She slept with Cassius?"

"He never said." I sighed. "He never admitted it. The child was — not normal."

"Not normal?"

"She wasn't a vampire."

"What was he?"

"I don't know," I whispered. "Perhaps I'll never know — maybe that was Cassius's way of protecting me, of protecting my bloodline, my reputation, though it hardly mattered once everyone discovered my mate was suddenly dead."

"But..." The green of her eyes started to fade. "Is that what would happen to me if I left you?"

"No." My hands shook holding her down; from showing her the memory, my strength had been depleted. If I didn't feed, I was going to sleep for the next fifteen hours. "Humans are turned immortal after they produce a child, a gift we bestow upon them."

"So she should have lived."

"I killed her before she could accept the gift because Cassius was right. She was going mad with a lust for power. Had I given her immortality, I would have created a monster."

"You still killed her."

"I loved her too much to let Cassius do it — loved her too much to turn her into a monster. She wasn't made for it. She was one of the first humans to start... showing effects of the imbalance. A part of me believes it's my fault that the humans keep dying."

"What are you saying?"

"No human mate had died — until I killed my own mate."

"And then?"

"Every human after... has died — not right away. Most live past a hundred having not aged at all. We think the immortality takes, and they simply don't wake up."

"You did something," she whispered, "to the natural order."

"Possibly."

"So it's your fault."

Heaviness descended like a fog. "It was my fault... for loving her too much."

"Your love for her destroyed everything."

"So now you know." I moved away from Genesis and laid

my head down on the pillow next to her. "Loving again will take everything I have left."

"You can't love again? Or you won't?"

"It's already too late…" I slurred my words, darkness overtaking me. I needed blood and sleep. "It's too late for me now… but not for you."

"What?" Genesis shook my body. "What do you mean?"

"If you don't love back, the final step never completes itself. You'll be free. I'm setting you free."

"Ethan." Her voice was distant. "Ethan, what's happening?"

"Exhausted." I barely got the word past my lips.

Something soft hit one of my fangs. And then blood was trickling into my mouth.

Memories flashed.

"Now it's your turn to dream," Genesis whispered. "Dream of me."

Blackness overcame me and then, in an instant, I was sitting in a desk with other humans listening to the instructor drone on and on about immortals.

"Never look an immortal in the eye!" the teacher snapped. "You are nothing. Remember that."

I cringed.

A bell rang in the distance. I watched as Genesis stood and walked out by herself.

Her mother was waiting for her at the end of the hallway, hands on hips. "Where's your backpack?"

"Oh…" Genesis covered her mouth. She couldn't have been older than seventeen. "I totally forgot. I'll go back to my locker and—"

"Do you really think any immortal will want you? If you can't even remember something as silly as a textbook?"

Genesis shook her head, tears welling in her eyes.

"Useless." Her mother gripped Genesis's arm and shoved her the rest of the way down the hall. "Good thing your number will never be called — you're too ugly."

"Yes, Mother."

I wanted to scream in outrage. She was gorgeous! Even in the dream, I could see the purity of the blood, taste the goodness on my lips.

A house appeared in the distance.

It was poorly lit. The shutters were falling from the windows, and the porch steps had seen better days. The foundation crumbled beneath the heaviness of the home, making it appear depressing.

I took the steps two at a time and found myself in Genesis's room.

She had books everywhere. Books about vampires, werewolves, and sirens. Then finally, Dark Ones.

"Are you studying?" Her mother's voice sounded from the other side of the house.

"Yes!" Genesis yelled, tugging a piece of licorice through her teeth. "Almost done for the night."

Her mother appeared at the door, took one look at Genesis, and scowled. "Candy makes you fat."

The licorice fell from her lips as tears welled in her eyes. "I thought you said I could have licorice if I skipped breakfast?"

"Ugly." Her mother sighed. "And now you'll be fat for them."

"But a number hasn't been called in years!" Genesis argued.

Her mother stilled. "Are you challenging my authority?"

"No." Genesis hung her head. "I'm sorry."

"I do this because I love you."

Bullshit!

Instead of staying in Genesis's room, I followed her mother to the other room where she sat down at a kitchen table and started pouring over bills.

Most of them were overdue.

"Stupid girl," she said under her breath. Her hands shook.

I glanced harder into the mother's eyes.

Jealousy stared right back.

"My number wasn't called." Her mother sniffed, still talking to herself. "Of course hers won't ever be called. It's all because of that *stupid bitch."*

She wasn't talking about Genesis.

Confused, I moved away from the mother and made my way down the hall again. Pictures lined the walls.

I smiled at the pictures of Genesis as a child.

Something about her struck me as familiar. Almost oddly so.

Her mother was in one picture.

And then another elderly woman. She had pretty, almond-shaped eyes.

The pictures went on, years and years of pictures. The color turned to black and white.

When I reached the end of the hallway, there was one final picture.

It was ancient. I leaned in.

My knees buckled as I braced myself against the wall.

"Ara," I breathed.

CHAPTER TWENTY-FOUR

Genesis

HE SLEPT FOR HOURS. I STAYED. A part of me wanted to leave, but he was right. After ten minutes, I'd calmed down enough to think about the situation logically, not that I still wasn't terrified he'd end up killing me. I no longer felt safe, but I didn't feel like Ethan was a threat.

I'd used his fangs to drop blood into his mouth, hoping it would have the same effect, since he was going to sleep. I wasn't sure if it would help him understand me better, but if it was a night for sharing, maybe he could at least pull information from my past.

I wasn't confident it would be helpful. He'd probably be bored out of his mind, but it was worth a try.

Two hours after giving him my blood, he jolted awake, nearly sending me off the bed in fear.

"Ara," he yelled.

I flinched. "Ethan? You were dreaming. It's okay." Clearly, my blood hadn't worked.

He turned, his eyes predatory. "Tell me you didn't know."

"Know what?" I brought my knees to my chest. "What are

you talking about?"

"She's from your bloodline."

"Who?"

"Ara."

"The mate you killed?"

He growled.

"I—" Tears welled in my eyes. "Are you sure?"

"Her picture." His eyes went black. "I saw a picture. It was old — it was her."

"You have to believe me." I held up my hands. "I would never lie."

Ethan shook his head; dark circles appeared under his eyes. "Sorry..." He trembled. "I'm still exhausted. It was a shock. We need to visit your mother."

"She hates me."

"Shall I kill her for you? Once I've gained the information I need?"

"No," I blurted.

Ethan sighed against my neck. "Just give me the word if you change your mind. The woman's insane."

"Ara?"

"No. Your mother."

"I hope it doesn't run in the family."

"Your blood is pure." Ethan kissed my neck. "Believe that truth, and you'll be fine."

"Is that—" Insecurity wrapped itself around me. "Is that why you wanted to mate with me? Because I remind you of her?"

"No!" Ethan pounced on me, his eyes so black that I was afraid if I stared too long I'd fall into their depths and never come back to reality. "You're different — you feel different."

"Different," I repeated.

"Better," he soothed, nipping my lower lip. "The best."

"I don't want to be her."

"You aren't." His voice was commanding. "And I'm too

exhausted to spend the night arguing with you."

"You can take more blood… if you need to." The thought sent a little thrill of excitement through me as his eyes faded back to green.

Ethan moved off me and stared up at the ceiling. "You don't want me to do that."

"Why?"

"Because," he growled, "it won't be a little blood, just like it won't be a little bite… just like I won't stop at the bite but will continue kissing you and possessing you until you can't breathe — until my body fills yours, until you scream for more just when you don't think you can take it."

I had no words.

"Scared you?"

"I'm not sure." Was I feeling fear? Or excitement?

"Your heart's racing."

"Yes."

"If I asked you for everything, would you give it freely, knowing what you know?"

"If I offered you everything, would you take it? Knowing the possibility of my bloodline?"

We lay in silence.

I thought Ethan had fallen asleep.

Until he moved, hovering over me, his lips grazing mine with the softest of kisses. "I don't think I can stop myself…"

"What?"

"I can't set you free. I know I said I could. I can't. I lied."

"A vampire who's a liar. Who would have thought?" I teased.

He didn't return my smile. "It's a death sentence."

"Then show me sweet death." I wrapped my arms around his neck. He let out a pitiful groan before his mouth touched mine again.

"You ask for death — yet you offer me life."

"I'm human. We're confusing like that."

His smile felt good against my lips.

"Kiss me harder," I begged, hooking my legs around his body.

"I'm old... go easy on me." He returned my frantic kiss with a slow torturous one of his own. He licked my lips then pierced the bottom, sucking away droplets of blood.

"You don't want easy." I sighed.

In a flash, I was on my back, my shirt completely gone. "You're right." He tongued the curve of my ear. "Mine."

"Yours."

My jeans went flying. "All. Mine."

Cold air bit at my skin. My heartbeat sped up as Ethan's body hovered over me, his lips hot on my neck. With a growl, he tugged my hair, forcing my head back, exposing my neck completely to his lips.

His fangs slid across my neck. "I'm going to mark you forever. You still have a choice, Genesis."

"No," I breathed, squeezing my eyes shut, "I really don't."

"You do," he urged. His body was scorching hot behind me. "Tell me no."

"I can't," I repeated, tilting my head back further, arching my back.

With a growl, he pierced my skin. I felt each drop of blood leave my body.

I reached for his shirt, but he slapped my hands away, pinning my wrists above my head as his mouth nipped my neck again. My body almost bucked off the bed when he drank more. It was different than before.

His tongue scalded me — in the best way — almost like he really was forever marking me, making it so anyone who looked at me knew whom I belonged to.

"Ethan—" I almost choked on his name, stunned I could even remember it after all the emotions swirling inside me — fear, excitement, lust, and something else, something bigger than me, bigger than him, having him pressed against me, his hot mouth on my skin. It was right, even though I couldn't explain anything beyond that.

He drank deeper.

The room exploded into a burst of light.

I gasped in response. His mouth left my neck and moved along my chin.

He released one of my hands. I immediately dug it into his hair and pulled his mouth to mine. Our mouths met with such aggression — almost violence — that I was sure more blood would be drawn.

He chuckled against my lips. "Is the need for me greater than anything else?"

"No," I lied, not wanting to admit to him that my need was so great I didn't even want to survive without him — couldn't.

His eyes darkened as his tongue slid across my mouth. "I can taste the lie on your lips."

"Really?"

"God, you're beautiful." His eyes were so black, so inviting.

I tugged his head again then moved my hand down his chest. He closed his eyes; a hiss escaped between his teeth.

He lifted the shirt over his head and grabbed my hand, holding it firm against his muscled stomach. "Touch me."

I really didn't need an invitation.

I don't know what possessed me to lean forward and lick his stomach — but that's what I did.

A guttural growl erupted from him as soon as my tongue licked along the thick lines of muscle along his stomach. "I said touch me. Don't kill me."

Laughing, I traded licks for kisses; he tasted sweet — scalding. Power surged through me with each tremble of his body, each moan. His hands dug into my hair, tugging me closer to his chest. I reached for the button of his pants, expecting him to slap me away or say something.

He went very still.

Too still.

Nervous, I pulled back and looked up at him.

His eyes were back to green. "There's no going back, Genesis."

I kept my gaze trained on him as I slowly undid the button and slid my hands inside.

Green turned to black as his fangs dug into his bottom lip. His head tilted back. He was like a god... in that moment more immortal than I'd ever acknowledged or realized.

CHAPTER TWENTY-FIVE

Ethan

HER HANDS STOPPED MOVING.

I'd killed her.

That was my first errant thought — because at that point, I'd stopped thinking rationally and had moved past logic, straight toward possessing Genesis and marking her beyond recognition.

With a groan, I touched my forehead to hers gently, so as to not scare her into realizing that she was, in fact, ready to give herself fully to something not human.

Her breathing picked up speed again.

I smirked and moved her hands down the side of my hips. When her fingers came into contact with my length, she let out a tiny gasp.

"Care to explore?" I taunted. "Or does the human not like playing with fire."

She gripped me — hard, almost painfully so — considering I was ready to impale the poor thing.

"I can handle it," she whispered in a husky voice.

"Prove it," I smirked, licking her lips again, needing that

taste more than I needed anything else in my existence.

Her tight little fingers began to move. I enjoyed her innocence for about two seconds before I was ready to lose my mind.

"What?" she asked when I moved her hands away and quickly ripped off the remainder of my clothes. "I thought you wanted me to explore."

"We'll explore later," I said gruffly.

Her cheeks stained with delicious blood.

"I'm not patient," I blurted. "Not when it comes to you — your taste." I lunged for her. "Your essence."

With a predatory growl, I tugged her shirt down and bit between her breasts then licked my way down toward her navel. Her body was made for exploring for hours on end — hours I didn't have — because selfishly, waiting seemed like a horrible idea.

Each lick had her muscles clenching.

Each kiss, her body damn near flying off the bed.

She was sensitive to my every touch. Possessiveness washed over me as I moved down her hips and bit the inside of her thigh, where her life source — her blood — ran purest.

I received a kick to the head. Dodging it, I chuckled and bit the other side of her thigh.

"That... feels... funny." She gripped the sheets in her hands.

"I believe, in this situation, the correct word is amazing... not funny, humorous, or any of the sort," I growled.

"S-sorry." She tried clenching her legs together.

"No." I pulled them apart and gazed upon every inch of her. "You're mine. I get to see every inch of you, I get to lick all of you, and when I'm done, I get to taste over and over again until you scream for me to stop."

"You think I'll want you to?"

I barked out a laugh. "You're only human."

"Don't break me."

"Wouldn't dream of it," I whispered against her inner thigh. "Now let the vampire play."

"I'm not sure I'm capable of handling that without passing out," Genesis whimpered when my mouth found her core. She let out another gasp while I steadied her hips exactly where I wanted them. She tasted so sweet I could have died.

"Ethan!"

I pulled back. "That was more of an irritated yell, not a scream." Sighing, I replaced my hands with my mouth. "Try again, human."

Tremors wracked her body.

She clenched her eyes shut. When they opened, they were bright green.

"Ethan." Now she said my name like a prayer.

"Yes?"

"What's happening?"

I was making sure she never left me — that's what was happening. "You're ready for me..."

"No." She shook her head. "I don't think I can take anymore of—"

I took possession of her mouth then lifted her into my arms. My lips moved to her neck, and I bit, knowing the effect it would have on her.

Our lovemaking wouldn't be fast.

Not if I drank.

I was going to extend every sensation... in slow motion.

One drop of my own blood lingered on my tongue. I shared it with her just as our bodies joined together.

Genesis's green eyes blinked in wonder as I lowered her down on me, inch by inch, sensation by sensation, each second sharing another drop of my blood, slowing down the process and making it so she would never forget what it felt like to be with her mate — to be possessed by me and only me.

Her body was made for mine — stretched around me so perfectly that even in my old age, with my experience, with my patience, I refused to share more drops of blood, refused to drink anymore. I just wanted her. Over and over again.

"You're mine," I demanded, thrusting faster and faster. "Say it!"

Her nails dug into my back.

I needed to hear the words.

Her green eyes flashed. "Ethan."

"Say it..." I slowed.

"Don't stop."

"Say it!"

"I'm yours."

The words washed over me as I thrust one last time, the walls of my carefully built world crashing down around me in shattered pieces.

She gave me her body.

In return, I gave her my soul.

CHAPTER TWENTY-SIX

Genesis

MY BODY WAS HEAVY — ON FIRE — and the only way it felt better was when I was pressed against Ethan. I had no idea how long we'd slept. He woke me up three times in the middle of the night. Each time, he'd drunk from me, never a lot, but enough to make it so my world stopped.

Each kiss was like a slow drug.

Each touch of his fingertips, each caress, went on for an eternity until I lost complete track of time.

I fell asleep with my face pressed against his solid chest and my legs wrapped halfway around his body.

"Genesis." His smooth voice was hypnotic. "Genesis, wake up."

"No." I pressed my face harder against his chest.

A warm chuckle erupted. "Yes, we have work to do. Well, you have work to do, and then after your so-called work, we're going to pay your mother a visit."

I didn't open my eyes. "No staying in bed all day?"

"About that..." Ethan sighed. "The good news is it will feel like we've been in bed for days when really it could have been mere hours."

"Hmm?" I perked up. "Well, that's a nice trick."

"I'm full of them." His eyes sparkled. "Care to know more?"

"Yes," I whispered, my mouth finding his.

With a groan, he pushed me back against the mattress and loomed over me, his naked body glorious-looking against the sunlight streaming through the window. "Perhaps we'll stay a bit longer."

"Yes." I nodded my head eagerly. "I'm your mate, after all. Don't you want me to be pleased?"

"You were pleased at least four times last night, possibly five, if we count the time I—"

"Shh." I put my hands over his mouth.

He smirked. "Afraid the dust will hear?"

I rolled my eyes.

"Ethan!" Alex's voice boomed on the other side of the door. "Feed her!"

"Ignore him," Ethan hissed.

The knock got louder. "For the love of God, she's human. Give her food."

"He's a siren. He knows nothing." Ethan continued kissing me.

"Mason will break down the door if he has to." Fighting broke out in the hall. "Ethan, I can smell the sex from here. One immortal to another, feed her before you can't feed from her anymore."

Ethan growled and pulled back from me. "They have no manners."

I was half-tempted to cover my face with my hands. Had they heard us? Of course they'd heard us, and they knew, and they could... Yeah, I wanted to crawl under the bed and hide for a few days. Instead, Ethan pounced from the bed, put on a pair of jeans, and jerked open the door while I tried to hide beneath the covers.

Alex peered over Ethan's shoulder and waved.

I had no choice but to wave back and hope that I wasn't as red as I felt.

"She's alive." Alex held up his hand for a high five. "No? Not funny? Too soon?"

"Horrible joke," Mason said next to him. "I made eggs. She's going to need food. Make her eat everything on the plate and—"

He was still talking when Ethan slammed the door in his face and brought a giant plate of food over to me.

"Forgive them." Ethan scowled. "There aren't typically secrets between us, and they're just concerned for you."

I pointed at the eggs, ten slices of bacon, and toast. "Clearly, they don't want me to starve."

"Wolves." Ethan looked heavenward. "He should be more concerned with his own diet, the ass."

"It does smell good." I moved up the bed so I could lean against the headboard. "Do you eat?"

Ethan's lips curved into a predatory smile. "I ate several times last night. Care for me to refresh your memory?"

My cheeks burned.

"So tempting." He reached for a piece of bacon and held it to his lips, taking a small bite that had my entire body clenching to keep from reaching out and attacking him. "And yes, I can eat. I typically do eat but haven't been because when we drink, we don't need normal food."

"But before me..." I grabbed a piece of toast. "You were eating normal food."

"I like you better." He winked. "But yes, I was."

"Good to know I'm better than bacon."

"Your taste..." His eyes brightened. "...is unlike anything I've ever had."

"Hmm..." I licked my lips.

"Stop it," he hissed and looked away. "Damn, I can't watch you eat. I'm going to shower while you eat your entire plate as per Mason's orders, and then I'll contemplate letting you leave this room so you can go to the bookstore."

"Ah!" I almost knocked over the food. "My job! Am I late? Will I get fired?"

Ethan burst out laughing. "It's eight in the morning. He's expecting you when I drop you off. No sooner, no later. You won't get fired. He wouldn't dream of it, and you really are adorable."

"And hot." I sighed.

"That too."

"No, I mean hot, as in, it's scorching in here."

Ethan winced. "You may be that way for a few days."

"Hot?"

He nodded.

"Why?"

"Too much vampire blood makes you overheat a bit." He shrugged. "It won't turn you— You're very much human, like I've said before, but sometimes the vampire blood causes a type of burn to take over in your bloodstream, not painful, just not exactly pleasant if it's a hundred degrees outside."

"Good thing it's Seattle." I bit into the toast.

"Yes, well, I imagine at this point, raindrops would simply turn to vapor if they landed on your skin."

I smiled.

"Shower." He nodded. "I'm going to turn around now and walk away."

"Narrating?"

"Apparently, that's what I do when I can think of nothing more than ripping that sheet from your body, slamming you into the nearest wall, and possessing you all over again."

I dropped the toast.

He growled, taking two steps toward me, then swore and turned back around.

"Have a good shower!" I called.

Another growl was his answer, and then his jeans went

flying. I wasn't laughing anymore.

THE RIDE TO THE BOOKSTORE was torturous. Ethan pulled over a half-dozen times just to kiss me. It was noon by the time we actually made it there, and even then, I almost refused to get out of the car.

"Four hours," Ethan repeated for the tenth time. "Do your work, contribute to society, enjoy yourself, and after... we'll make a visit to your mother."

My stomach dropped to my knees.

He gripped my chin between his fingers and kissed my mouth softly. "We need to know the truth, Genesis."

"Why?" My voice trembled.

"Because it may have something to do with the prophecy, or it could just be a rare coincidence. I swear, I won't let her hurt you."

I sighed, already drawing into myself.

"My offer still stands," Ethan whispered.

"What?" My head snapped up. "What offer?"

"I'll kill her," he said softly. "All you need to do is ask it — and it's done. She doesn't deserve life for the way she treated you, and it would make me happy to see you hold your head high around her."

"But she'd be dead."

"Perhaps I'll just toy with her a bit."

I giggled.

"Go." He kissed me again. "And if Cassius shows up—" Ethan swore. "Which he may, considering he's insane and has a death wish... try to ignore him."

"Done," I answered. "Besides, I could touch him all I wanted..."

Ethan growled.

"...and still crave you."

His face softened. "I wish that was true."

"It is."

His face was sad. "I'll see you in a while."

CHAPTER TWENTY-SEVEN

Genesis

DRYSTAN'S EYEBROWS SHOT UP TO HIS hairline when I walked into the store. I wondered if all immortals could smell what I'd been doing — or where I'd been. Then again, Ethan had said he'd marked me.

So maybe it was just like walking around with his scent all over me.

"Genesis." Drystan pointed to a stack of boxes. "We just received another shipment. Why don't you put the books away to start off with, and then I'll have you help customers."

"Great." I reached for the boxes and was surprised when they didn't feel heavy at all, maybe it was compliments of the vampire blood which was currently making my veins feel like they were on fire.

Ethan had said it would wear off throughout the day, but my body still felt hot. I wasn't sweating, but I felt like I should be.

I carried the stack of boxes over to the corner and started pulling out books. Each one was in alphabetical order, making it easy to find a spot on the shelf for them.

I was halfway finished when I felt it — the chill in the air.

"Cassius," I breathed, "didn't take you for a reader." I knew I was safe from him as long as I didn't touch him. I was bonded with Ethan, meaning, at least part of Cassius's charm was going to be lost on me.

He chuckled darkly. "How'd you know it was me?"

I turned, welcoming the relief the cold of his body brought me. "You're chilly."

"I am that." He nodded, shoving his hands into his jean pockets. He looked almost human. His dark hair was pulled back from his face, tucked behind his ears. His eyes appeared more gray than white, and he was wearing a perfectly harmless combination of jeans and a white T-shirt.

He still looked huge.

And completely out of place in society.

Then again, people probably assumed he was an NFL player or something.

"Did I pass inspection?" He grinned.

I rolled my eyes and turned away. "Have any good dreams recently?"

"Are you saying you miss my invasion, sweet?"

"No." And I didn't. I was just curious, more curious about him than I cared to admit, especially after everything Ethan had shown me. My hand caressed the spine of the book I was placing on the shelf.

"Questions... Perhaps I should sit down." He pulled a chair from a nearby table and sat, folding his arms over his chest. "You may begin when you're ready."

"Arrogant," I snapped.

"Feisty." He sighed cheerfully. "Always happens when you have a bit of spice in your blood. Vampires aren't known for their calm demeanors."

I licked my lips. "What happened to Ethan's daughter?"

Cassius stilled, his breathing stopped altogether. "So he's shown you... That's brave of him, all things considering."

"Mates don't keep secrets."

"Oh?" His voice dripped with doubt. "I must have missed that lesson in the last two thousand years."

I couldn't hide my shock. "Two thousand years."

"Give or take a few days." He shrugged. "Ethan's daughter was not Ethan's daughter. I took care of the situation as I saw fit. Don't forget who I am, human. Or what I am and what that means for you and your pitiful fleeting little life."

I swallowed and backed away. "Are you threatening me?"

"Think of it as a reminder," Cassius whispered. "When all this is said and done... if you fail, if Ethan fails, you'll be just another blip on the immortal life. A mere... *memory*."

"Great pep talk," I muttered, reaching for another book.

"I didn't sleep with the human," Cassius offered. "I know that's what you're thinking. What type of friend... or brother... would do such a thing? Did I kiss her, try to win her affection? Naturally, because that's the order of things in our world. If she cannot stay strong for her mate, she doesn't deserve immortality."

"So you test all the humans?"

"Yes." His voice was final. "And if they fail..."

"They die."

"They're simply eliminated before the natural order of things happens. Eventually they die. Take Mason's mate, for example. Lovely girl, obsessed with the wolf — dead."

My eyes burned with unshed tears. "Ara..." I hated saying her name. "She didn't love Ethan."

"In her selfish heart, I believe she thought she was in love with him. She loved him in the best way she knew how. She loved herself more."

I nodded, sadness piercing my chest, making it hard to breathe.

"More questions, or shall I simply touch you and be done with it?"

Ignoring him, I shoved another book in its place.

"Stephanie says you aren't bad."

He said nothing.

I thought he'd left, but when I glanced over. He was staring into the space above my head as if in a trance. "Stephanie." Her name sounded different on his lips. But as soon as he'd uttered it, he closed his eyes and shook his head as if he didn't want to talk about it anymore.

"I'm not bad." His eyes turned white. "But I'm not good either."

"What? So you just hang out in the middle?"

"When it suits me." He smiled then stood. "Tell me, do you believe yourself strong enough to resist a Dark One's touch?"

"I did before." I stepped back from him. "Before I was mated to Ethan."

"His blood makes you strong. His mark... stronger than before." Cassius tilted his head. "But the human heart is the strongest of all. It surpasses all immortal claims."

"My heart is my own."

Cassius sighed, his eyes sad. "And that is the problem with humans, is it not? They continuously lament not being able to find love, and when they do, they still refuse to relinquish their most prized possession. Oh, they give their bodies, their souls, but their hearts?" His chest almost grazed mine. "They keep for themselves."

"Why?" I blurted.

He stilled, tilting his head to the side, making himself look more predatory, like an animal ready to pounce. "Fear."

A gasp escaped my lips.

"Fear," he repeated, "is not welcome here."

And suddenly my world made sense.

"I wonder," Cassius whispered, his breath freezing the air in front of me, "when the time comes, will you also choose yourself? Give into fear, or finally sacrifice the one last shred of humanity you have in order to gain immortality?"

I opened my mouth to answer.

"About done?" Drystan called then appeared around the corner.

My lips were freezing, probably blue, but Cassius was nowhere to be seen.

"Genesis?" he repeated. "Are you alright?"

"Yes." I found my voice. "Fine. I'm almost done."

"Good."

He walked back around the corner. I lifted another book just as the barest of whispers flew past my ear.

"Until you sleep…"

CHAPTER TWENTY-EIGHT

Ethan

I KNEW HE'D VISITED HER THE minute her eyes met mine. She should still be on fire for me; instead, she felt — warm.

Yet her heart still pounded for me. That was all that mattered. That's what I told myself as I gripped the steering wheel and drove us toward her mother's residence.

"Cassius." I hated that she said his name with such familiarity. "You said he's like your king?"

"Mmm-hmm."

"Who does he report to?"

"The archangels." I sighed. "When they care enough to check in on us."

"Are they bad?"

"Humans — and please don't take offense to this — like to categorize things so they can better understand them. If something is bad, they stay away. If it's good, it must be safe. But is chocolate really good? Perhaps to you, but what if someone's allergic? What's worse, what if you gorge yourself? Then something that was once good in your eyes is suddenly very bad because it has the power to kill you. The same goes for immortals. Are all Dark Ones bad? No. But they aren't good. Are archangels bad? Yes. In a way they can be very bad, but they also have such goodness that it's blinding. What you should concern yourself with is not trying to understand, because you never will."

Genesis let out a frustrated sigh. "Easier said than done."

"If I told you he was bad," I reached for her hand, "you may stay away longer, but it may also cause fear to grow in your heart, and fear is not an emotion I want you to feed."

She nodded. "I'm afraid now."

"Of me?"

"My mother." Her eyes were distant, locked on the house I'd just pulled up to.

It looked better, as if someone had made repairs. The shutters no longer fell from the window, and the porch had been rebuilt.

"Say the word, and I end her life," I vowed. "Now hold your head high."

Genesis nodded wordlessly and followed me out of the car to the door.

Her mother was by herself; I picked up only her scent. I knocked.

Footsteps creaked against the wood floor. And a short woman with graying brown hair appeared in the door. Her eyes were bland, her skin wrinkled. Life had been hard on her, or maybe that was humanity's punishment for being such a horrible mother.

Her eyes met mine, widening briefly before settling on her daughter. Her smile was full of venom. "So, you're his whore now?"

With a hiss, I shoved the woman into the house and walked her backward until she was against the nearest wall. I gripped her throat with my hand, lifting her until her feet dangled beneath her.

"Say it again," I dared her.

Tears filled her eyes.

"What? Trouble breathing?" I tilted my head. "Care for me to end your miserable existence?"

She croaked out a *no*.

I released her then whispered in her ear, "Disrespect my mate one more time, and you won't even feel the slice of my teeth across your throat."

The woman paled.

Genesis's hand gripped mine, steadying my heartbeat, when all I wanted to do was rip her mother's throat out and laugh over her dead corpse.

"Mother." Genesis trembled next to me. "We won't be long. I just had a few questions."

"Knew you would." She snorted. "But I don't have answers for you, at least the ones you're looking for."

I moved away from Genesis, walked down the familiar hallway, and located the picture. I pulled it from the wall and tossed it to her mother. "This woman. Who is she?"

Her mother's face paled as she stared at the picture. "Dead."

"Caught that," Ethan hissed. "Who is she?"

"Ara was her name." Genesis's mother petted the picture as if she was reliving something. "Everyone hated her."

I tensed.

"She was beautiful, and she knew it... so vain that she made the family look bad. Her number was called, but of course it was. The rest of the families were jealous. And then she failed."

"Your great-grandmother?"

"Great-aunt." Her mother set the picture down on the table. "She's a stain upon the family name. We don't discuss her. This is the first time our number has been called since Ara's disgrace." She snorted. "And I knew it would happen the minute Genesis was born — that skin, that hair." She rolled her eyes. "So beautiful, just like Ara."

Genesis's heart thumped wildly, so loudly I had to concentrate on what her mother was saying in order to hear the words above the beating.

"I made her strong." Her mother's eyes met mine. "Better she hate her own reflection than fall prey to it."

"How tragic," I whispered, "that you felt the need to shame a little girl for having golden hair and pretty eyes."

"It worked!" her mother screamed. "Look! Mated to an Elder! A vampire, no less!"

"It worked," I repeated, "because her blood is pure... because her soul is pure." Anger crashed over me at her mother's proud expression. In a flash, I moved behind her, biting a small mark on her shoulder and whispered, "For the rest of your days you, will see nothing but Ara's reflection when you look in the mirror. You will hate, and it will drive you mad. That is the gift I leave with you for bestowing such kindness upon the woman I love."

Her mother swayed and then fell to her knees. A tear fell down her cheek. "No, please no. Don't do this."

"It's done." I gripped Genesis hand. "We'll bother you no more."

Genesis didn't want to follow me; her feet dug into the ground, so I tossed her over my shoulder and carried her out of the house.

When she still didn't make a noise, I buckled her seatbelt and peeled out of the parking spot, driving like hell back toward our home — toward safety.

Ready to lose my mind, I opened my mouth to apologize when she blurted, "You love me."

"If that's what you wish to discuss..." I reached for her hand.

She squeezed mine. The heat from my blood took over, making her skin hot to the touch.

"And you won't leave me? Ever?"

"No," I vowed. "I don't think I'm capable of surviving

such a loss."

She nodded, wiping a tear from her cheek. "Cassius visited today."

"I know."

She sighed. "He told me things… about you. About Ara."

"Did he touch you?"

"No," Genesis whispered. "But one day soon, he will. He touches all the human mates."

I scowled. "So he told you…"

"To test them."

"Yes."

"I'm going to pass."

"Alright."

"You don't believe me?" She pulled her hand away.

I sighed and focused on the road ahead of me. "I have no reason not to believe you."

Genesis let out a loud sigh. "Do you think the only reason you love me is because I'm related to Ara?"

"No." The entire idea was ridiculous. "Not only was she horribly selfish — something I've finally come to terms with — but you're nothing like her. Besides, you don't stop and stare at yourself every time you see your own damn reflection."

"Thanks to my mother," Genesis mumbled.

"That's it." I pulled the car over, forced it into park, and reached for Genesis. With a growl, I tugged her body across the console and into my lap. "She did you no favors. That woman was no mother to you. A weaker female would have crippled beneath that type of emotional scarring. I should have killed her for what she put you through."

Genesis's eyes pooled with tears.

I cupped her chin. "Beautiful inside and out — the last thing you need to be is afraid of your own beauty. Embrace it, but don't let it overtake all sense of reality. You are beautiful. You are strong. You are pure. Those are simple facts. Outside of that, nothing else matters other than the way I feel about you."

"If being beautiful means I turn into Ara, I'd rather be ugly."

"You could never turn into her." I pressed an urgent kiss to her mouth. "You're... *you*."

Genesis returned my kiss, biting down on my lips.

I flicked her tongue with mine then deepened the kiss. "Home."

"Bed."

"Yes," I growled, rubbing my body against her. "Now."

She let out a little gasp.

"Or here." I tugged her shirt over her shoulder, kissing the bare skin. "Vampires can be very... creative."

"Show me." Her eyes burned bright green.

I ripped the rest of her T-shirt with my teeth. "Never... challenge me."

Frenzied hands reached for my jeans while I reached for hers, both of us colliding with one another as we tried to peel clothing away.

Layer after layer went flying.

And then she was naked, straddling me.

"Mmm..." I took her fingers between my teeth. "...I've never tasted anything so incredible."

"My hands?"

"Your skin." I chuckled then placed myself near her entrance. "You know... we could always wait until we get home and—"

She welcomed me into her body.

But didn't move.

I let out a frustrated growl and gripped her hips. "You think to tease me?"

"I was told never to tease a vampire."

A mixture of laughter and ecstasy left my lips as our bodies began to move.

"No bite this time?" she asked.

"Sometimes," I growled, thrusting hard, then pulling out, "faster is better."

CHAPTER TWENTY-NINE

Genesis

WE MADE IT HOME.

But I was without shirt, considering Ethan had ripped mine to shreds. So he handed me his while he walked into the house sporting a pair of jeans and a really big smile.

"Ethan." Alex was in the kitchen drinking wine and reading. "Is today no-shirt day? Should I remove mine as well?"

He reached for the edges of it but earned a growl from Ethan.

Mason was sitting in front of a bowl of berries; his hand paused midair as he looked between the two of us. "Damn, Ethan, at least feed her every once in a while."

"He's very concerned with food, always concerned with food." Alex nodded. "Hurry up, Mason, your berries are drying out."

A berry went flying by Alex's head.

I didn't notice Stephanie in the corner; she wasn't normally so quiet. When her eyes met mine, they lit up. "Hey, how about shopping tomorrow? Before your fun little human job?"

She looked like she'd been crying. "Are you okay?"

"She's fine," Alex snapped, his good humor completely gone. The room turned tense in an instant. He cleared his throat and forced a smile. "Sirens, very emotional."

Stephanie smiled. "Very."

"Ethan, a word?" Alex stood.

"Sure." Ethan kissed the top of my head and left the room while Mason started rummaging around the kitchen; pots and pans clanged together, and then he pulled out a giant piece of steak.

"I hope that's not for me." I pointed.

"Protein..." He threw the steak into the pan. "...feeds the blood, which feeds the mate, which, in turn, feeds you."

"You gonna start singing Circle of Life?" I joked.

"Circle of life?" he repeated.

"*Lion King?*"

"Cassius is king."

I looked helplessly to Stephanie, who was trying to hide her smile behind her hand.

"Have you seriously never watched *Lion King?*"

"Werewolves are scared of TV," Stephanie said with a soft laugh.

"And sirens are afraid of the dark," he fired back, while she shuddered. "I'm not afraid of the TV. I just don't see the point in sitting in front of a flat box and watching people make fools of themselves."

"He'd rather be the fool." Stephanie nodded and winked in my direction.

"Mason..." I walked over to him and put my head on his shoulder. "How about I eat the steak and we watch *Lion King?*"

"No."

"*Dances with Wolves?*"

Stephanie snickered loudly behind her hand.

"Wolves do not dance," Mason growled.

"Oh, we know." Stephanie nodded. "I've seen it once. Don't care to see it again."

"Too much whiskey." Mason kissed the top of my head. "Eat the whole steak, and then we'll talk about King Lion."

"Lion King."

"Same thing."

I sighed helplessly and went to sit at the table while Mason cooked.

Stephanie gave me a side hug. "Eight tomorrow morning, alright?"

"Great."

"Bed." She shrugged. "It's been a long night." Her eyes misted again.

"Are you sure you're okay?"

"Yeah." Her voice cracked. "Like Alex said, we get emotional. Can't help it."

It felt like she was lying, but I was human, how would I know? I nodded and turned my attention back to Mason, who'd started searing the steak.

"So you cook meat but refuse to eat it?"

"I'm a vegetarian." He smiled. I'd never realized how pointy his teeth were on the sides. Maybe that's how he'd been able to bite into me before Ethan had mated with me.

"Your teeth say otherwise." I pointed. "Flat means vegetarian. Pointy means carnivore."

Mason rolled his eyes. "I didn't say it was natural for me to be a vegetarian."

"Okay... so why?"

He let out a heavy sigh. "Meat made my mate sick... for one reason or another. It gave her headaches. She only ate fruits, vegetables, nuts." He flipped the steak. "So I learned to like other foods."

"And now?"

He went very quiet, his eyes focusing in on the steak.

"Now…" His voice was hoarse. "I honor her with my every meal."

My throat clogged with emotion.

The fact that he honored her at all — but with every single meal — killed me. How did he survive that? How did he live every day having known true love? And know he may never experience it again — living forever?

"Don't pity me." Mason let out a gruff growl. "It makes it harder."

"Sorry," I whispered. "So pinecones, huh?"

He laughed. "Yes, well, it's an acquired taste."

"I bet."

My heart picked up speed, and then I smelled him. Ethan entered the room, briskly walking by me, kissing my head. "Steak almost done?"

"I'm a perfectionist." Mason held up his hands. "Let the juices seal."

Ethan scrunched up his nose. "Her blood tastes better than that steak."

"Yes, well, her blood tastes good because she's living. She's living because I feed her."

"Werewolf has a point," I teased. "Besides, if I eat my whole steak, we're going to watch *Lion King!*"

"Whose king?" Ethan tilted his head. "What lion? Mason's a wolf."

And that's how I ended up spending my evening between a vampire and a werewolf, eating steak and watching a Disney movie while they argued over the animal kingdom, not to mention the lion's choice in song.

It felt right.

Like I'd finally found my place.

My home.

I had no idea that the security I felt was about to get ripped from me, from the very people I'd put my trust in.

CHAPTER THIRTY

Ethan

I TRIED TO WATCH THE CHILDISH movie. I even engaged Mason in an argument over the silly cartoon, but my thoughts were elsewhere.

On Alex and Stephanie.

On what he'd just revealed to me, betraying his own sister's confidence because he was so damn worried about what she would do — what she was capable of.

"She thinks she loves him," Alex muttered sourly. "Yet she doesn't wear his mark. It's as if he's refused to mark her, but she still... craves him."

"Sirens crave sex," I mumbled. "You know this."

"This is much different." Alex shook his head. "Something's shifted, I don't know what... but..."

I pinched the bridge of my nose. "He wouldn't dare mark her for death. Immortals don't mate with each other — not in that way. It's not natural."

"That's what I said."

"We can talk later." I sighed. "I'll try talking to her."

"Thank you." Alex's body slumped against the chair. "I

worry more than I should."

But really, his worrying was merited because Stephanie wanted what was forbidden for her to want.

A Dark One.

Our king.

To want him was to invite death.

And I wasn't so sure she would listen to any of us, regardless of how wise our words, our warnings. The heart, I'd learned in all my years of living, wants what it wants, and damn the rest of the world for trying to tell it otherwise.

Genesis fell asleep in my lap. I carried her to bed then hovered protectively over her, instinct kicking in. I would die for that girl. I would do anything for her.

I wasn't sure she felt the same.

I doubted myself and hated that I doubted myself.

She stretched her arms above her head. She looked like a cat, all seductive and curvy. "Ethan?"

"Yes?"

"Why are you watching me sleep?"

"Because you fascinate me when you dream."

"I don't want to dream of him." She reached for my body, tugging me against her. "How do I keep him from getting in?"

"You don't." I sighed helplessly. "Just know you're safe in my arms. You'll always be safe."

"But in my dreams I'm in danger?"

"Remember what I said about good and bad... the same goes with danger. When all else fails, Genesis, you follow your heart."

"The heart can be evil."

"Not yours." I shook my head. "Never yours."

"I'm going shopping tomorrow."

"I know." I chuckled. She was so tired she wasn't making much sense. "Stephanie will charge whatever you want to my card."

"Too much money."

"I'm rich."

"Because of the fish."

I laughed. "Yes, the fish. They make me rich. Sleep, little human." I kissed her nose as she wrapped her body around mine and fell into a deeper slumber.

I waited, unable to sleep until I felt the cold seep from her body into mine.

Her breath staggered.

And then her skin went from hot to cold.

"Cassius," I whispered, "you take her from me, and I'll rip your heart from your chest."

"Trust her," he said back to me.

Agony washed over me as I waited for Genesis to return. Every second that went by was torture because I knew it was another second he was tempting her with forbidden fruit.

Just like he'd tempted Ara.

Only Ara had bitten.

And with that one bite, destroyed a part of myself I'd never been able to get back.

Until now.

CHAPTER THIRTY-ONE

Genesis

"IT'S SNOWING." I HELD MY HAND out and caught a few snowflakes. "No lake today?"

Cassius shrugged. His mood was different, darker. "I wanted the comfort cold brings me."

"Normally it's heat."

"I'm the opposite of warmth." His eyes turned white. "Therefore, it's cold that comforts. It's my fire."

I pulled the fur blanket around me. We were sitting outside a cabin in front of a roaring fire. It was beautiful; snow-blanketed the forest, making it seem enchanted.

"More questions…" Cassius sighed. "I sense them."

I stared into the fire. "What was Ethan's daughter?"

"Different question," Cassius snapped.

"Can you mate?"

Cassius let out a slew of curses. "Our punishment or maybe our prize? Women die at our hands. Human women." He shrugged. "Vampire blood and human blood co-exist. Angel blood and human blood are an abomination."

My throat went completely dry. "So it can't mix."

"It can... for a time, and then the angel blood overwhelms what weakness the human has. It makes them evil, destroys them from the inside out."

"So you can't mate."

"We don't mate," Cassius snapped, "because there is no point, Genesis."

"That's lonely."

His eyes closed. "You have no idea."

"What about other immortals. Can you mate with them?"

"Why risk more lives?" Cassius threw a piece of wood into the fire. His eyes still hadn't returned to a normal color — they were void of color, void of emotion. "Is that it for this evening?"

"One more..." I held my hands out to the fire.

He nodded.

"Is there a way to test the prophecy? To make sure it works?"

"There is always a way," Cassius sneered, "but I highly doubt it is a road you want to travel — or one your mate would let you even step foot on."

"So I wait to live or die?"

"You pass all tests, you live — and hopefully restore balance. The prophecy says a human will mate with an immortal. It will be the new beginning, and they'll have a child."

I shuddered. "I don't want to die."

Cassius's eyes met mine. "Then don't."

"Wha—" He disappeared in front of my very eyes.

And then I jolted awake, shivering in Ethan's arms.

"What did he do? Meet you in a freezer?" Ethan swore, gathering me against him, wrapping blankets tightly around my body.

"S-sorry." I shivered. "I didn't realize how cold I was."

"He thrives on the cold." Ethan rubbed my shoulders. "And clearly forgets himself if he put you in the middle of a blizzard."

"It was a snowstorm... I think... but pretty."

"Oh well, as long as it was pretty," Ethan hissed.

I tucked my head against his chest, focusing on his warmth. "We need to have a child."

Ethan's hands stopped moving. "Cassius told you that?"

"It's part of the prophecy, right?"

"Yes, but—"

"So that will make it come true, right?"

"No," he said, sadness evident in his tone. "I wish that were true, but no, Genesis, we won't know until..."

"I no longer exist." I trembled. "He said there's another way—"

"No!" Ethan yelled. He gulped in a breath released it then said more softly, "No, it isn't an option."

"Maybe if you told me."

"It's forbidden."

I pretended to be satisfied with that — but I wasn't. If there was a way to fix the balance of things, I was going to find it. Not just for me, but for Ethan — for Mason, who'd lost the love of his life — for Cassius, who seemed lonelier than Death.

If I could save them—

I had to try.

CHAPTER THIRTY-TWO

Genesis

"READY?" STEPHANIE POPPED HER GUM AND hooked her arm in mine. "Ethan gave me his credit card with no limit, meaning we have damage to do."

I nodded, forcing myself to smile. Something felt... *wrong*. I'd spent the night in Ethan's arms, yet I felt like my balance was off, like I was straddling a line and was about to get pulled over to the wrong side.

Stephanie directed me toward a white Lexus hybrid and practically shooed me inside.

"So I'm thinking Downtown, since it's close to work."

She nodded. "Work? Why would you want to work anyway? I'm just curious."

I shrugged. "I need a purpose."

"But Ethan is your purpose."

"Right, but Ethan has a job too. It's not good to be idle, you know? Plus, I'm not really good at anything... other than reading... so why not work at a bookstore? It helps out Drystan, and so far I like it."

She snapped her gum and shrugged.

Her hair was pulled back into a ponytail, exposing her neck. I was about to glance away when I noticed a mark on her neck.

"Did someone bite you?"

"Lovers all bite..." She smiled. "If they're good."

"Oh."

"Hey, relax. We're shopping. This is fun. You get to spend your mate's money, and you get me as your personal shopper for the next few hours."

I forced myself to smile and embrace the moment. "You're right."

"Course I'm right." She turned up the music and started singing at the top of her lungs.

By the time we'd made it downtown, we only had a few hours until I had to be at work.

Shopping with Stephanie was like an Olympic sport. She took me from store to store, tossing clothes in my empty arms and ordering me to try them on before I'd even told her I liked them.

She knew my style well. Not fussy, comfortable — but cute. I tried on several pairs of jeans, bomber jackets, shirts, boots — the list went on and on. I needed more coffee if I was going to make it through the rest of the day without passing out.

Or maybe I just needed Ethan.

He would be nice too.

"Hey!" Stephanie knocked on the door to the dressing room. "Hurry up in there. We only have a few more minutes."

I rolled my eyes and stared at my reflection. "Can I ask why you put me in a black evening gown?"

"Because!" She laughed. "Ethan will want to show you off."

"Fine." I pressed the heavily beaded fabric against my stomach. It was strapless and ridiculously heavy. Black with silver beading cascaded from floor to ceiling, it seemed.

I was like a walking pageant queen. "Stephanie, I don't think I like this."

No answer.

"Stephanie?"

With a sigh, I opened the door. Words died on my lips.

"Hello." His white eyes matched his long white hair. He tilted his head to the side as if examining me. "Come."

I stepped back and shook my head. "Where's Stephanie."

"Come." He held out his hand. His body was massive, bigger than Cassius and Ethan combined. He stood at least eight feet tall. Why was no one else running and screaming? He was beautiful, but it was a deadly type of beautiful. I don't know how, but I knew if I touched him, I'd die.

When he ducked into the dressing room, I gasped, covering my mouth.

Wings. He had wings.

Gold feathers that appeared then vanished right in front of me.

Ethan! My mind screamed.

Cassius... he could read my thoughts; he was powerful enough. I started yelling for him in my head, hoping he was tracking me, hoping in vain he would be able to find my scent. There was no way I was escaping the immortal in front of me.

"You're an archangel," I whispered.

"And you're the human."

Not *a* human. *The* human.

I gulped. "Please don't make me go with you."

His smile widened. "Are you afraid?"

It felt like a test.

I didn't know what to say.

I opened my mouth to yell no, but it was like he'd stolen the words from my lips. His head tilted back. "Come."

I shook my head, forcing myself to breathe, to not give into the fear that threatened to choke me.

"Come, or I kill your vampire. Your choice."

My throat released. "Don't!"

"So you'll come?" He seemed pleased.

"Just don't hurt him."

"You have my word. It won't be me who hurts your mate."

I nodded and reached out, touching my hand to his. And my world faded to white.

CHAPTER THIRTY-THREE

Ethan

"SO THINGS SEEM TO BE PROGRESSING nicely." Alex smirked over his morning coffee.

Ignoring him, I rolled my eyes and continued reading the paper. I was just about to put it down and grab my keys so that I could finish what I needed to do for the day and find an excuse to stop at the bookstore, when pain sliced through my chest.

My knees buckled as I reached for the table to steady myself.

"Ethan?" Alex was immediately by my side.

My blood boiled, turning to acid beneath my skin as the room started to spin. "Something's wrong."

"Sit down."

I pushed him away.

Mason was soon at my other side.

The door to the house opened, and Stephanie appeared right in front of us. "Ethan, I tried to—"

Our eyes met.

Hers were white.

"What. Have. You. Done." I roared, the heat in my blood searing every rational thought in my body.

Stephanie held up her hands and took a step back. "Nothing. I did nothing. I woke up, and she was gone!"

Alex cursed. "Cassius."

"No," I repeated. "It isn't Cassius."

I would feel Cassius — I'd felt him before when he'd taken one of my mates, knew the way it felt when my blood turned to ice in my veins.

"Stephanie?" Alex's eyes narrowed. "Your neck."

Growling, I pushed away from both men and slammed her against the granite countertop, tilting her next to the side so severely I was surprised her head hadn't come off.

"No." Hands shaking, I stepped away. "No."

Stephanie rubbed her neck; tears streamed down her face. "What? What's happening?"

Her eyes were still white.

"Did you see… it?"

"See what?" She was nearing hysterics. "Something knocked me out, and when I woke up, she was gone!"

"The archangel," I said in a hushed tone. "You wear his mark."

Stephanie's horrified gaze met mine as she started vigorously rubbing the spot I'd just discovered. It was small, white, and had the appearance of a snowflake tattoo. It would have been beautiful if it hadn't been a mark of death.

"No." She hugged her arms to herself. "I'm so sorry. I thought we were safe. We should have been safe."

"Can you track her?" Mason growled next to me, his body trembling with the need to change and tear something limb from limb.

"Yes," I said in a voice I didn't recognize. "But it may be too late. I'm strong enough to fight him, to distract him, not strong enough to defeat him alone."

The room fell silent.

Pride kept me from saying his name.

But my love for her trumped everything.

So in that moment at my kitchen table, I closed my eyes and uttered a plea — to my greatest enemy.

"Cassius," I whispered, "help."

CHAPTER THIRTY-FOUR

Genesis

MY TONGUE FELT LIKE SANDPAPER IN the roof of my mouth. When I tried to lick my lips, it was like someone had dehydrated me then handed me peanut butter.

I tried moving my lips. They were heavy, pressed together.

"You won't speak."

I blinked my eyes open. Having already thought they were open, I was surprised when I saw a blinding light appear in front of me then fade into the darkness surrounding my body.

"I allow you to speak after you've earned it." It was the same man or angel as before. His feathers were now fully visible; pieces of every color of the rainbow shimmered from the large wings, though his seemed to favor purples and blues. It seemed like that should be significant, the colors, but I couldn't talk, so instead I stared, knowing I probably wouldn't ever see anything like it in my entire life.

I wanted to be afraid.

And I was.

But I was also fascinated by the sheer beauty of the archangel in front of me. Long white hair, which should have looked stupid and old, created an ethereal effect around his sculpted face. His eyes were a bluish-white, more aqua than anything, and his mere presence filled up the entire room.

"Are you afraid?" He tilted his head to the side, his eyes studying me for a reaction.

I didn't nod.

I simply stared back.

"I'll take that as a no." His full lips curled into a smile. "I am Sariel. I've been watching you."

Creepy statement. I shivered. The last thing I wanted was a being like him watching me.

"It intrigues me..." His smile grew as the light faded around his body, making him look more human than immortal. "How they fight over something so insignificant."

I flinched.

"I don't mean you, little human." He moved around the room. Lights followed each footstep until I realized I was sitting in a large open room — a lot like a typical living room with couches and tables — facing the Puget Sound.

It would be normal...

If an archangel wasn't walking around in front of me, glowing all over the place.

"The situation — it's insignificant. Tell me, why should my brothers — why should I bother myself with the prophecy? It does not directly affect me."

He waved at my mouth.

My lips pulled apart. I inhaled then spoke. "It may not affect you, but it affects others. People are dying — what if I'm the answer?"

He turned his back to me. "Do you think that we would put the balance of immortal lives in the hands of a mere human?"

"Yes," I whispered, "because it's the only thing that makes

sense."

"You speak to me as if you have the right to breathe in my presence without falling to your feet in terror."

"And you speak to me like you deserve to be worshipped, when you've done nothing but kidnap me and mock me."

His body stilled.

I blamed Ethan's blood. I'd spoken out of turn. And I was going to pay for it.

"Keep that heartbeat under control. Wouldn't want that vampire blood to boil you from the inside out... quite painful I've heard, the process of a human turning immortal."

"What?" My heart raced. "But I'm human."

"Yes." He turned back to face me. "For now you are human. Until the choice will be made by the immortals. You will stay that way, in my care."

"Why?" I gulped. "Why take me?"

His shoulders hunched; it was the only chink I'd seen in his armor the entire time we'd been talking. "Because once, a very long time ago, one of my sons made a great lapse in judgment, and the immortals have been paying for it ever since."

Sariel folded his hands in front of his large body, his wings going once again transparent. "Because of his sins, a darkness — a sickness — descended upon both races. I mean to rectify that in the only way I know how."

I was afraid to ask.

"Well?" he smirked. "Aren't you the least bit curious?"

"No."

"Lie." His eyes flashed white. "Blood will be spilled. They will come for you."

"And if they don't?" I whispered.

"Blood will spill either way."

Was it my imagination, or did his eyes hold a hint of sadness?

"Balance always needs to be restored, and you, Genesis,

will be tested. I wonder, are you strong enough to do what needs to be done?"

I gulped. "What needs to be done?"

"Telling you defeats the purpose, now, doesn't it?"

"So I'm your prisoner... until blood is spilled?"

"Think of it as a vacation." He shrugged. "I've provided for all of your needs." He pointed to an open kitchen I hadn't noticed before. "You won't starve, you won't thirst — unless it's blood your body craves — and you have a view. What more could you want?"

"Is that a trick question?"

His grin blinded me. "I enjoy humans... so small."

My eyebrows knit together in frustration. "Thanks."

"...and interesting."

"You said you had sons." I tried changing the subject.

His face shadowed. "I have... sons, yes."

The conversation must have been over because he quickly walked out of the room.

I thought he'd left me alone...

Until someone or something walked in. I wasn't sure how I knew since I hadn't actually seen anything, but I felt something.

And then I heard chains.

I had a brief vision of watching *Christmas Carol* and shivered, sitting on the nearby couch and pulling my knees to my chest. "Hello?"

"Hello." The voice was smooth, like a caress against my face.

The couch sunk next to me.

A hand reached out of the air. I followed the fingertips up an arm; the body slowly came into focus.

It was a man. Not an angel.

A Dark One — or something else entirely.

He had chains around his feet, though clearly he'd still been able to walk, and his hands were chained together as well.

"I'm Aziel." He leaned back against the couch. "I hope you're stronger than the last human who visited."

"The last human?" I repeated.

"She looked like you." His eyes went cloudy as he stared out through the windows, his jaw set in a firm line. "The same blood flows through your veins."

"She died?" My mouth was like cotton. I wasn't sure how much more I could take.

"She was murdered." His teeth snapped. "I would have made her my queen."

I tried to scoot away, but he put his chained hands onto my legs, holding me in place.

"She was tested," he sighed in a cheerful voice, "and found lacking."

"Why was she tested?"

"Because she wanted too much — because it was within our capacity to give it to her — but we were too early. The prophecy never said when balance would be restored. And we are not perfect."

We?

"We are still flawed." His voice was hollow. "And we were wrong. I was blinded by her face... then again, I've always had a fascination with pretty things." He turned his head to me. "You remind me of her."

I flinched, trying to move my body to the side. His hands grew heavier and heavier on my lap.

"And you will probably die just like her."

CHAPTER THIRTY-FIVE

Ethan

"THE LAST TIME YOU CALLED FOR me was over a hundred years ago," Cassius said from behind my spot in the kitchen. I'd been pacing for the past ten minutes, waiting for him to arrive.

Stephanie and Alex tried to get me to feed.

I didn't want blood from a bag.

If I couldn't have her — if I didn't have her — I wanted nothing. Death. I would welcome death.

"She's gone." I didn't recognize my own voice. It was hoarse, like I'd been choked and barely survived. "An archangel—"

Cassius moved by me and held up his hand, his eyes blazing white for a few seconds before he uttered a curse. "Sariel."

Mason whistled and fell down into a chair, hanging his head in his hands. "We should have kept better watch of her. We should have—"

"Mason..." I shook my head. "It wasn't your fault." I turned my attention to Stephanie. "Care to explain how you earned the angel's mark?"

Cassius's head craned to the side, his eyes so white they almost glowed. He stalked toward Stephanie then with one hand pushed her up against the wall, pulling her head to the side to glance at the mark. "Decided to whore yourself out?"

Stephanie's face paled. "I had—"

"Do not lie." Cassius dropped her to the ground. She crumpled against the floor, holding her head in her hands. "He didn't say he was going to hurt her."

I lunged for her.

Mason intercepted me.

"He said she needed to be tested. You all knew there was another way." Slowly, Stephanie inched to her feet. "If an archangel deems the human pure, he'll restore balance, regardless of the prophecy!"

"And that worked out so well last time," Cassius hissed.

Lost, I simply waited for someone to explain. When nothing happened, I pretended to lose my irritation. Mason's arms slackened. I lunged for Stephanie's throat, my fangs hovering over her artery. "What. Exactly. Did he promise you?"

Her heartbeat picked up.

"Worth dying for, siren?"

"Love always is," she whispered.

It wasn't a lie.

I stepped back. Tears filled her blue eyes. "He promised me Cassius."

Cassius went completely still next to me. The room temperature plummeted, causing a frost to cover the granite countertops. "So, you thought to enslave me?"

"No!" Stephanie sobbed. "You said we could never be together... immortals do not mate. I simply—"

Cassius held up his hand. It shook in the air, and pieces of frost fell from his fingertips. "You would betray a defenseless human — one for whom we have been waiting for over a hundred years — because you think yourself in love with me?"

The room began to freeze; pieces of ice formed along Cassius's face, shattering into the air the minute he opened his mouth to speak. "Dark Ones do not love."

A tear slid down Stephanie's cheek, freezing against her porcelain skin. "But we've spent nearly every night together."

"And every morning I spend with someone else," Cassius said in a flat voice. "I didn't think you were becoming so attached as to sell your soul to an archangel in order to align your destiny with mine."

"But—"

"Enough," Alex barked. "Stephanie, stop… you're making it worse."

Cassius hung his head. "You can track her blood?"

"Yes," I hissed. "But going up against Sariel…"

"He's old," Cassius stated in a bland voice. "Older than me."

"Not hard," Mason grumbled.

Cassius snapped his teeth together. "The only way to rescue her, to pull her away from the archangel's scent, would be…" He looked up, his eyes flashing once again. "…to mix the blood."

"Yes." My voice shook. "She needs angel blood."

"She won't take it." Cassius shook his head. "Believe me."

"She has no choice!" I yelled, pain searing my limbs, making them feel heavy. "She either drinks from you and makes the choice to leave, or he'll keep her forever. You know he will."

"He does like his toys." Cassius swore. "Unless he truly believes she's the human we've been waiting for, and then things are about to get a lot worse."

Alex pushed Stephanie into a chair and crossed his arms. "How can it get worse?"

"Death," I whispered. "We can distract him long enough to grab her, shield her from his scent. But if he truly believes what we do — then blood will be spilled."

"For balance to be restored." Cassius sighed. "Blood always needs to be spilled."

"Does it matter who?" Alex asked. "Because I vote Stephanie."

Her soft sobs were grating on my nerves. I should have watched her closer — should have seen the signs of her infatuation. Dark Ones did not mate for a reason. They were too addicted to those who fell for them, destroying the other half that should help make a whole.

"Track her," Cassius finally said. "We'll go when he's at his weakest."

Night.

Sariel taught the stars how to shine. At night his resources were depleted on account that his power was shared with the sky.

"Alex..." I nodded toward the siren. "Keep her locked up until we return. And Mason?"

He stood. "Let me go with you."

"You're not strong enough." I hated saying it, almost as much as I hated that I was right.

Mason let out a growl.

"Wolf..." Cassius put his hand on Mason's shoulder. "Your diet makes you weak. Therefore, it makes us vulnerable. You stay."

I knew it hurt Mason's pride.

His eyes went completely black as he slowly sank into the chair, his face completely tight with outrage. Berries and cones didn't make a werewolf strong — he knew that as much as we did.

"Ten miles away." I sniffed the air for traces of the woman I loved — the woman who was taken from me. Anger overtook all good reason as I started moving toward the door.

"Level head, Ethan." Cassius's cold grip stopped my blood from boiling over. "She'll need you at your strongest."

"I know."

"Drink."

I had to have heard him wrong.

"Drink." His teeth snapped. "Before I change my mind."
He lifted his hand to my lips.

With a sneer, I pushed him away.

He slammed me against the wall. "You want to save your
love? Stop being so damn prideful and drink."

With a hiss, I bit into his arm and sucked deep. His blood
was like ice, cooling my veins, making my body so calm I was
finally able to think clearly. I took a step back, the blue tint of
his blood dripping from my fangs. "I won't thank you."

"And I won't expect it." He moved his fingers along the
small indents. The skin slowly closed back together.

"If she touches you—" I whispered.

"When she touches me," he clarified, "you will finally see
it."

"That you were right all along?" I growled.

"That you should have trusted her to begin with."

CHAPTER THIRTY-SIX

Genesis

AZIEL SAT WITH ME FOR WHAT felt like hours. Sometimes he spoke, but mostly he rocked back and forth. It didn't make me feel better.

When I tried to get up and grab something to eat, he told me that the food was poisoned.

I didn't know if I should believe him or not.

I got up anyway because I couldn't handle just sitting and staring out the window, even though that seemed to be his own specialty.

I found a bottle of water in the fridge and drank, then made my way back over to the couch. Sariel hadn't returned. I wasn't sure if Aziel was supposed to be my guard or just a punishment.

"What's with the chains?" I asked, taking a seat next to him, careful to be out of his reach just in case he decided to put the same hands in chains on top of me, forcing my legs to go to sleep.

"A punishment." His eyes went white as snow. "For my sins."

"What did you do?"

"I wanted."

"What did you want?"

His hair became more visible. Pieces of black and white tendrils fell across his face. "I wanted."

"Okay…"

"Haven't you ever wanted so desperately you'd do anything to have it?"

That was how I wanted Ethan, but it wasn't just want. To say want almost seemed selfish — I needed him.

Just thinking about him had my heart racing. My entire body trembled with a need to just be in his arms.

"I wanted," Aziel continued, "so I took."

"And you were punished?"

"Very much so." Aziel nodded. "I can no longer fly." He shrugged. "I'm grounded with chains, and now I must watch history on repeat until the balance is restored."

"Until humans stop dying," I clarified.

"Yes."

"Is it me?" I was afraid to ask but needed to know. "Will I bring balance?"

"We could have waited to discover the truth." He ignored my question. "Better this way — to get it over with. I pushed Sariel to pursue it, though he'd deny my involvement. I smelled her on you. And I knew we needed to try."

Great. So I had two people to blame for my captivity.

"Soon." Aziel faded into the air briefly before flickering back. "Very soon now."

The sun had already set, casting a pink glow across the sky.

Ethan was out there somewhere… I wished in that moment I could communicate with him, tell him not to come for me. I didn't think it was a trap, but something in my gut told me things wouldn't end well, and I'd rather sacrifice myself than see him hurt.

I swallowed the fear.

Cassius had made sense when we'd talked earlier.

Fear was selfish. It kept me thinking about me and not about others. It kept my heart safe, because if I stayed afraid, I wouldn't risk losing.

But for Ethan? I would risk it all.

My life.

My soul.

My heart.

"So the Vampire has decided to work with the Dark One." Aziel clapped his hands together, shooting me an amused grin. "Perhaps you *are* worth the trouble."

Sariel walked through the door, eying Aziel briefly before making his way toward me. "They're close. Shall we begin?"

I took a step back.

"Fear?" He smiled mockingly.

"Let's try excitement."

His mocking smile faded into a real smile. "Ah, that's better."

"What?"

"I can see why my son was so enraptured with you."

"Aziel?" I guessed.

Sariel glanced to the couch and shuddered, "No."

"Then I'm confused."

"My son..." His eyes went from blue to icy white. "Cassius."

CHAPTER THIRTY-SEVEN

Ethan

CASSIUS WAS IRRITATED THAT WE HAD to drive, but not everyone could simply appear out of thin air. Part of his angelic heritage made it so that he could, in essence, fly, though he preferred not to discuss it with anyone. Just another reason Dark Ones couldn't be trusted. There were parts, dark parts, they kept hidden that we would never understand.

His blood continued to ice my veins, taking away some of the pain at having Genesis ripped from me.

I'd only experienced this type of pain once before.

When I'd had to kill my own mate.

It had taken me fifty years to stop craving her.

Every evening when I went to bed, I'd dream of her only to wake up in a cold sweat, craving her taste, her smell — everything about her.

The only way to exorcise it from my system was to starve myself of blood, allow her blood to leave my body. It was a battle, possibly with my own bitterness at her betrayal.

"He will not kill her," Cassius said once we reached the Sound.

I snorted. "You think that's what I'm worried about right now?"

"Yes."

I looked away, clenching my teeth, unable to speak because I hated that he was with me, hated that I needed him at all.

"I never took your mate," Cassius said in a detached voice. "I tested her. I never stole her from you. Her betrayal was not my fault."

"You still touched her," I whispered.

"After she begged me," Cassius fired back. "You know I would never force myself on a human."

"You took my mate and my daughter."

"I will say this only once," Cassius growled. "You have no daughter."

"She was more mine than yours."

Cassius ignored me and continued driving. "When we arrive at the house, try your best not to charge the archangel."

I rolled my eyes. "You make it sound like I have no self-control."

"When it comes to Genesis, I believe self-control is something you seriously lack, brother."

"I love her."

Cassius sighed, a slight frown marring his face. "Yes, I know."

"What do you know of love?" I spat, clenching my hand into a tight fist, my knuckles cracking against each other as I fought to keep my rage at bay.

"I know," Cassius said in a hoarse voice. "Believe me when I say I know."

I didn't point out that Dark Ones didn't love — that love was just as forbidden as mating, just as ridiculous a notion. They felt no love because they gave themselves over to their angelic blood more than their humanity, and everyone knew angels didn't feel, didn't love.

They simply existed and ruled, but never by such human emotions. To feel such strong emotions was the reason the Dark Ones had been cursed in the first place.

"Are we close?" Cassius asked.

"You truly can't trace her?" I was curious, with all his strength, how he couldn't pick up her specific smell. From where I sat, I could even make out her heartbeat.

"No." Cassius sighed.

"There." I pointed at a large house facing the Sound. It was a two-storied beach house; intricate brickwork lined the front. A door big enough for two angels to fit through loomed in front of us.

"Well?" Cassius shut off the car. "Shall we?"

I grunted.

It would be impossible to catch Sariel unaware. He was an archangel, not necessarily all-knowing, but most likely expecting us. What mate wouldn't fight through hell to gain his love back?

We walked in silence toward the door.

I wasn't surprised when it opened.

My heart beat wildly in my chest as the scent of Genesis became stronger, her heartbeat more erratic.

"Easy," Cassius said under his breath.

I clenched my teeth together.

The solid oak door opened before our very eyes. A blast of humidity shot through the air making me hold my breath as the sting of sweet sugar invaded my nostrils. It smelled of angel—of the heavenlies. I wondered how Cassius dealt with it—when my own body was already shaking with the need to run in the other direction. Because that very smell was the one I'd always been warned about. *If it smells too good, it is too good—run.*

Suddenly the archangel appeared, his wings dripping with purples and blues as his feral face tilted to the side, a smirk lining the corners of his mouth.

"Sariel." Cassius smiled, of course he would. "I think you have something that belongs to the vampire."

"But of course." Sariel nodded. His wings fluttered as he looked me over with a calculating glare. His head tilted to the side. "Vampire, your love for her, is it pure?"

"Yes." It hurt to speak. I could feel her presence. I just wanted to see that she was all right, take the fear away, give her my blood, and get her the hell out.

"Mmm…" Sariel nodded to both of us. His eyes were blazing white. He wasn't just immortal, he wasn't human, wasn't man — more being or spirit than anything else. "After you."

Cassius stepped in the house first.

I followed, my nerves on edge as I pushed past the archangel, not caring that I was being disrespectful to someone who could end me if he willed it.

I didn't turn around.

And maybe that was where my instincts were off.

I always turned.

Always smelled.

Always sensed.

But this, this I didn't see coming, because the minute I moved away from the angel, my eyes locked on Genesis.

Blood. So much blood. I reached for her just as a jarring pain stabbed me in the back.

With a curse, I stumbled forward. Warm blood oozed down my back, mixing with the icy blood Cassius had given me.

"No!" Genesis screamed. "Ethan!"

Cassius turned, his eyes horrified as he reached for my back, and pulled out a single purple feather dripping with red.

"And now…" Sariel pushed me to my knees in front of Genesis. "…we begin."

CHAPTER THIRTY-EIGHT

Genesis

I'D NEVER BLED SO MUCH IN my entire life. Just when I was about to pass out, Aziel appeared by my side and told me to drink. Whatever he brought me tasted funny. I tried to jerk away from him, but I was too weak from blood loss.

I heard Ethan's voice. My heart soared. He was there.

And then Sariel turned and offered a sad smile, almost as if he was apologizing for having made over a hundred different small cuts around my arms and neck.

It had happened so fast the pain didn't even register for the first minute, and then everything stung like a hundred fire ants had all bitten me at the same time.

"Genesis..."

Ethan had eyes for me and only me. I wanted to yell for him to stop because something wasn't right. Something felt very wrong. Cassius moved away from Ethan toward me, maybe to help, maybe to finish the job. When I saw Ethan stumble forward...

I knew.

Things were about to get a lot worse.

Cassius swore, pulling a feather from Ethan's back.

"Now we begin," Sariel said in a calm voice, picking up his pace as he stalked towards Cassius.

Confused, I watched as Ethan fell to his knees and reached for me, his face ashen, his eyes black.

"What did you do to him?" I yelled.

"Simply making him... a bit more human." Sariel shrugged, stopping directly in front of Cassius.

Cassius clenched his fists, his stance predatory. "It's been a while... Sariel."

"Father." Sariel shrugged, "And apparently I've been a horrible one... neglecting my children. Then again, you know all about being a father, don't you... son?"

In a flash, Cassius had his hands around the angel's neck. He threw him against the wall.

Sariel simply shook his body, his wings elongating to at least seven feet across. "I see I've touched a nerve."

"Ethan." Cassius growled. "Get her out of here."

Ethan shook his head then slowly stood and stumbled toward me. When his hand touched mine, it was slapped away by chains.

Aziel laughed. "No, no. The vampire watches. This concerns him, after all."

"Be silent." Sariel sneered, waving his hand at Aziel.

"Did you think you could bring the balance all on your own?" Sariel laughed mockingly, making my ears ring with its loudness. "Did you think that you were strong enough to shield all the immortals and humans alike from your sin?"

Ethan reached for my hand again, tugging me close to him.

My head slumped forward on his chest.

I didn't know if it was my blood getting all over him or his getting all over me. But I felt safe — finally.

Until Aziel lunged for me.

Ethan kicked him in the chest, causing a snarl to erupt

between Aziel's lips. "If I were whole, I'd rip you limb from limb — then again, I've already taken everything from you. Do you know..." He stood to his full height, which I hadn't noticed until now, matched Sariel's. "She gave me her body — her very soul — before you killed her."

Ethan shook in my arms, his fangs grazing my neck.

"And when I took her over and over again," Aziel laughed, "I promised her I'd make her immortal. If she did one tiny, little thing for me."

"Ethan, don't listen to him." I gripped the sides of his face. "Focus on me."

"Birth me a son," Aziel yelled. "And you know what that bitch did?"

Sariel had Cassius by the throat. With a growl, he punched Sariel in the chest, sending the angel soaring through the air again. "No!"

He was running toward us.

My mind wasn't putting the pieces together fast enough.

Aziel leaned down and whispered in Ethan's ear. "She gave me a daughter."

Cassius fell to his knees.

Sariel walked around him, pulling a long sharp feather from his wings. "One should never have to kill his own offspring."

"Cassius! Behind you!" I yelled.

Cassius hung his head like he wanted to die.

In a flash, Ethan's fangs were in Aziel's neck. He hunched over him, blue blood dripping from his fangs as he completely drained the angel.

When he stood, his eyes were white just like Cassius's. In two strides, he had Cassius by the neck and tossed him against the wall.

A crack ran from the bottom to the top of the ceiling as plaster fell from overhead.

"This is my favorite part," Sariel sang, removing himself

from the fight between Cassius and Ethan and coming to my side. "Where they are finally forced to finish what they started so long ago."

In my weakened state, I saw two of Sariel. I shook my head. "He can't die."

"Which one?" Sariel asked.

"Both." I forced the word out. "They'll kill each other."

"Ah, but balance must be restored."

"I don't understand," I whispered. "Ethan, stop!"

Cassius wasn't fighting anymore. It was like he wanted to die.

"Please!" I reached for Sariel, my fingers coming into contact with his soft velvet feathers. "Please."

"You know..." His eyes closed briefly. "That's the first time a human has dared touch me in... years."

"Sorry."

"It was warm." He sighed. "I've been cold for a very long time."

The air in the room shifted, turning to ice.

Ethan growled, his fangs nearly dipping into Cassius's neck when Cassius finally punched him in the jaw and stumbled backward. "I couldn't do it!"

"A daughter!"

"She wasn't yours!"

"You still killed her!"

Cassius fell to his knees. "No. No, I couldn't."

The room stilled as if someone had pressed pause on the TV.

"And so the truth reveals itself." Sariel put his arm around my shoulders. I was too weak to do anything but lean against his cold body.

"A daughter," Ethan hissed. "You would kill an innocent human."

"Abomination," Sariel said in a deadly tone. "Another Dark One. No Dark Ones have been born since Cassius —

since *my* sin."

Cassius flinched.

I wanted to hug him.

His own father thought him an abomination.

"No more Dark Ones must live." Sariel sighed. "And now that Aziel is dead, I am almost appeased. You see, balance was shattered the minute Cassius allowed the Dark One to breathe."

"I couldn't." Cassius shook his head back and forth. "She was innocent."

"So one of you will take her place." Sariel nodded. "One of you will take her place, and balance will be restored. It's as simple as that." He turned his head to me. "Choose, human."

"Wh-what?"

"Your destiny. You must choose."

"I don't understand."

"Who lives? Who dies?"

CHAPTER THIRTY-NINE

Ethan

ADRENALINE PULSED THROUGH MY BODY AS madness overtook me. All I knew was that I had to kill him — kill him for taking something important from me. But what?

"Kill, kill, kill," the voice whispered in my head.

Cassius wasn't fighting back. His eyes were white, haunted. It didn't register that he was giving up. I just wanted him dead.

"Dead, dead, dead," the voice continued to chant.

"Ethan, No!" Genesis screamed.

I wrapped my hands around Cassius's neck, ready to snap, ready to kill. When his eyes met mine, something had me pausing.

Why was I strangling him?

Why was I so upset?

I looked down at my hands, the same hands gripping his neck. Blue blood trickled from my fingertips.

"Damn it." I pulled back, chest heaving as my hands shook.

Aziel's blood was poison.

"Kill, kill, kill," his voice whispered. *"He took from us."*

"No." I fell to my knees, the blue blood continued to drip from my fingertips. I quickly bit into my wrist, letting more of the blood fall out of my system.

"Choose," Sariel said from behind me.

Cassius shook his head slowly. There was a piece I was missing, a piece of the puzzle that wasn't fitting together.

A daughter.

My mind replayed back the images. The baby was wrapped in a blanket — he or she wasn't human.

Half-angel?

A Dark One.

"Mine," Aziel whispered in my head.

"No." I choked out a hoarse cry. "You destroyed her."

Aziel would live until the last of his blood left my body. Images flickered in front of my eyes as if I was watching a movie.

Aziel crooked his finger at Ara. She didn't need any more encouragement than a flick of his wrist, a smile in her direction. Ara had been lost to him before she even took the first step in his direction.

"Wanted her," the voice whispered in my head. *"So bad."*

"You killed her." I hung my head.

"You killed her."

"Because it had to be done." I was arguing with a dead angel, arguing with the last of his lifeblood.

Cassius reached for me.

I gripped his hand and helped him to his feet. His face was covered in bruises. His lower lip bled blue. Dark hair mixed with blood caked on his cheeks.

"You didn't kill her?" I asked.

"Well done," Sariel said from behind us. "Didn't think a vampire could control himself, and now I see him touching a Dark One. Impressed, but this is going a bit too slowly for my taste."

The room went black.

A chill filled the air.

The last thing I heard was Genesis scream before the room flashed again.

Everything was in black and white.

The house around us faded to an apple orchard.

A little girl with bright blue eyes was climbing a tree, giggling as she went faster and faster.

"Keep up!" she yelled. "You can't catch me!" She laughed harder.

Cassius was standing beneath the tree, his hands on his hips. "Get down! You'll hurt yourself."

"Nope!" She hung upside down, her long hair nearly sweeping the grass beneath her.

Cassius grinned and grabbed her, setting her on her feet. "Remember to take your medicine."

She crossed her arms. "It tastes funny."

"I know," Cassius said in a low voice. "But it won't always be this way."

"Promise." Her eyes filled with tears, the blue flashing with such ferocity that it turned white.

"Promise," he echoed.

The scene changed.

The girl looked to be around twelve. The apple orchard was the same, only this time it was fall. Leaves were scattered around the grass, and she was reading a book.

"Boo..." Cassius stepped around the tree. "I've come to say goodbye."

"No!" The girl threw her book onto the ground. "Why? Why would you leave me?"

Agony crossed over Cassius's face. "You hardly see me as it is."

The girl hung her head. "It's my favorite part of the year. When you visit."

Cassius sank to his knees so he was at eye-level. "It's for the best. Besides, you have a brother to take care of."

"Yeah." She wiped her nose with her sleep. "He's cocky though."

"Heard that," a voice said from behind the tree.

Alex stepped into view and shared a serious look with Cassius.

"Please don't go." The girl wrapped her arms around Cassius's neck. "I'll miss you. You belong to me."

"I don't." Cassius choked out the words. "Now, run along and help your mother with dinner while I talk with your brother."

"Will I forget you?"

"No," Cassius whispered.

"You'll come back? One day?"

"Yes."

Satisfied, she ran off, leaving Cassius with Alex.

"You lied," Alex said, leaning against the tree.

"It's best this way." Cassius waved his hand into the air.

The girl staggered forward, scratched her head, and then kept running toward the house.

"The memories are removed. Just make sure she continues to donate blood and keep the glamour on her at all costs."

Alex shook his head. "I swear they'll never discover her true identity. On my life."

"Good." Cassius nodded. "That's good."

"Are you alright?"

"Of course!" Cassius pulled the hood over his head, covering his dark hair and white features, a pure giveaway to any of the townsfolk of what he was, what he was capable of. "Run along, Alex."

Alex rolled his eyes and left.

The girl stopped at the house, turned around, and lifted a hand in a cautious wave.

"Goodbye… Stephanie." Cassius cursed and walked in the other direction. Each step he took covered the grass with ice.

The scene faded.

And Ethan was back in the house with Cassius, Sariel, and Genesis.

Had they seen it too?

He turned to gauge Genesis's reaction. Tears streamed down her face as she shook her head in disbelief.

Cassius let out a pitiful moan.

"So you see…" Sariel rubbed his hands together. "…an abomination was allowed to live — still lives — for I've marked her, tasted her blood to be sure of it. Balance was wrecked the day she was born, and now we have someone from the same blood line living." He turned to Genesis. "Your great-great aunt should have made the call, should have paid for her sins. But she's dead, and soon Aziel's blood will leave your mate, and he will be gone from this world as well. So I tell you again, Genesis. You must choose who lives and who dies."

CHAPTER FORTY

Genesis

MY HEART WAS SHATTERING, BREAKING OVER and over again in my chest. It was hard to breathe.

Watching Cassius with Stephanie — it was like I could feel his pain, his agony as he watched her skip off — knowing that she would never remember him.

And things suddenly made sense. Why Stephanie was drawn to him. Why she loved him.

Why he pushed her away.

When all he wanted was to hold her close.

Tears streamed down my face at Cassius's helplessness.

Ethan looked absolutely dejected, his eyes black as he swallowed and gripped Cassius's hand.

It seemed, in the end, peace had been made between them. But who was I to decide? I loved Ethan, but I wept for Cassius, for what he'd gone through. I'd always been told Dark Ones had no capacity to love.

I'd been taught wrong.

Sariel, on the other hand, clearly had no heart — to put his son through that, to watch that and still ask me to choose who lived and who died.

I knew balance had to be restored.

It was my bloodline that had ruined everything in the first place. Ara had been selfish, and her selfishness had caused a split between our races.

But her selfishness had also caused a Dark One to love. And I couldn't be mad at her for that.

"Time's wasting," Sariel said in an irritated voice. "If you don't tell me, I'll just assume you wish for me to eliminate both of them."

"I love Ethan," I whispered. "But does that mean Cassius doesn't also deserve to live?"

"This has nothing to do with what Cassius deserves or your feelings for Ethan." Sariel pushed me forward. His feathers brushed against my skin. "This is logic, pure and simple. Two plus two does not equal three. For humanity's sake... for the sake of the immortals and keeping both races thriving... a life must be taken."

I trembled.

"You think me evil." Sariel's voice was so cold, so detached. "But this isn't evil. This is life and death. This is the most simple fact about both worlds — something that unites us, despite our differences."

"What about yours?" I asked. "What if I spilled your blood?"

Sariel's eyebrows shot up. "Interesting. You'd spill my blood to save them?"

"Yes."

"Impossible. But brave."

"A girl has to try."

He held out the purple feather. "Take it and make your choice."

My hands shook as I took the feather between my fingertips. How could something so soft be so deadly? The tip was pointed, like a knife.

"I love you." My eyes filled with tears as I looked up to Ethan. "You know that. You hear my heart."

"Genesis..." His eyes flashed. "Whatever you're thinking — don't. I can't live without you, but you can live without me." His voice cracked. "Cassius will take care of you, Alex, Mason..." His eyes pleaded with mine as a red and blue tear slipped down his cheek. "I'll always be with you." His hands reached out toward the feather, but Cassius moved him out of the way.

"I was the one who did wrong," he said in a strong voice. "I deserve punishment." His face cracked into a smile. "And I cannot love." His nostrils flared. "Even if I want to."

"But you did," I argued.

"In the past." Cassius eyes turned black. "And now I feel nothing."

"Lie." My voice was hoarse.

His breath hitched as he reached for the feather, his fingertips grazing the edges of it. "Genesis, stay with your mate."

Sariel hissed out a breath next to me.

"Sometimes it's best," I held the feather out. "To love for a moment than to never experience it."

"Genesis!" Ethan moved toward me just as Cassius reached for the stem of the feather.

I stumbled backward.

And pointed the edge directly into my own chest.

"No!" Ethan roared.

Sariel turned his back to both men, covering me with his wings as I fell slowly back, my heartbeat slowing in my chest until I didn't feel a beat anymore.

Sariel's face broke out into a smile as his wings blanketed my fall to the ground. His forehead touched mine, and with a brief touch of his mouth against mine, he whispered, "Fear is not welcome here."

"Not afraid," I choked out.

"I know." His eyes blazed white. "There is no greater sacrifice than laying down one's life for the life of a friend."

The room flashed white.

And I knew I was dead.

CHAPTER FORTY-ONE

Ethan

I COULDN'T REACH HER IN TIME.

My body screamed and a part of my soul, perhaps the last piece I actually possessed, went dead in my chest as the sound of her heart slowing brought me to my knees.

Dead.

I knew what death sounded like — and I'd just received the final blow of my existence.

Sariel disappeared.

Leaving her body behind. Her lips were blue as if the angel had infused his blood into her mouth before leaving me behind to pick up the pieces.

I let out a guttural moan. Tears streamed down my face. I couldn't hear her heart. I couldn't feel the warmth.

Heat seared my limbs as my blood boiled, killing any of the angel's blood still left in my system.

Cassius slowly walked over to her body and shook his head. "Humans… are not supposed to die for darkness."

I couldn't speak.

It hurt too much.

"Kill me too," I whispered. "Please."

Cassius's eyes flashed. "She wouldn't want that."

"She's dead!" I roared, charging him. "Just kill me."

Cassius flung me across the room. I stumbled against the farthest wall and charged him again.

With a flick of his hand, my body stilled. He'd frozen me, the bastard.

Vampire blood boiled to the surface, heating the ice.

"You'd do anything to get her back, but you take a chance she isn't the same." Cassius sunk to his knees. "You take the chance that you may lose her."

"You mean to make her immortal."

"Only I can bring her back from death."

I turned my head. "You know what your touch would do to her."

"Not with certainty," Cassius whispered. "No."

"She may become immortal — but forever be tied to you."

"But she would live," Cassius said. "It's your choice, but her heart stopped beating two minutes ago. We are running out of time."

The ice completely melted around me. I rushed toward her lifeless body and shook my head in disbelief. "I'd rather she live — a full life — a life she deserves, even if it's apart from me — than survive one more second with her light extinguished from this world."

Cassius nodded. "Grab her hands."

They were cold, so cold that her fingertips nearly burnt me.

Cassius leaned forward, his lips hovering over hers. Eyes white as snow, his face began to immediately heal as his mouth grazed hers, and then he whispered, "Breathe."

She was still motionless.

Blue lines made their way from his temples and neck toward his lips as he blew across her lips and whispered again, "Breathe."

His hand moved to her chest, and with one more exhale, he pushed down and commanded, "Breathe, human."

Genesis choked and then inhaled. I gripped her hands as hard as I could as her fingertips began to warm against mine. Body taut, I waited for her eyes to open, waited to see if they would be white like Cassius's — or green like mine.

She was breathing.

Her heart stuttered.

And then began to take off.

"Why aren't her eyes opening?" I yelled, reaching for her shoulders. "She's alive, she's breathing but—"

"I don't know." Cassius rubbed his face. "It's been a while since I've actually given immortality to a human." His eyes were no longer white but bright blue, his skin pale.

"I'm sorry." I choked on the apology. "I know what it cost you to do that."

Cassius said nothing, rubbing his hands together as if to ward off the chill of his own blood.

He would be weak for days, possibly weeks. After all, he was still part human.

"What do we do?" Her heart still beat, but color wasn't returning to her face.

"We take her home," Cassius whispered, "and wait."

I RODE HOME IN the back seat, Genesis cradled in my arms. I kissed her neck — I even bit, hoping my blood would help infuse some of what Cassius had given her of himself.

I was desperate.

I loved her.

And I refused to believe that she would stay in that state, comatose, unable to react to the world around us.

When Cassius pulled up to the house, Alex and Mason were already outside, running toward the car.

Alex opened the door first. "What happened?"

I couldn't speak. I just shook my head, holding her closer to my body as Mason shoved Alex out of the way and let out a guttural howl before changing in front of my very eyes and running off into the darkness.

"It's still fresh, the death of his own mate," Alex whispered.

With a nod, I slowly lifted Genesis up and got out of the car. Alex shook his head and glanced at Cassius. "Stephanie's been asking for you."

"Stephanie is dead to me," Cassius said in a cold voice.

I froze and turned slowly, ready to rip his head from his body. "She better mean more to you than you say, Cassius. It's because Stephanie breathes that Genesis sacrificed herself. Go. Now. Apologize. Tell her the truth."

Alex cursed. "No." He shook his head. "No. It would destroy her. It's been over a hundred years. Just let her believe the lie. It's better for everyone."

"She has no idea what she is!" I roared. "And Cassius saved her pathetic life only to have her turn over Genesis to the very archangel who commanded her death!"

Alex hung his head. "She's my sister."

"Not by blood."

"In every way that matters." Alex clenched his teeth. "You're asking me to tell her I lied to her my entire life? About what she was? About who she was? You know the best part? I weakened myself purposefully to keep her strong, to keep the glamour in place, and now you want me to take that all away? All those years?"

"Alex." Cassius held up his hand. "I should have never asked it of you."

"You are king," Alex said in a deadly voice. "You speak. We do. Regardless of right and wrong."

"And I was..." Cassius seemed to trip over the words. "...very wrong to ask you to limit your own immortality in order to shield people from what she was — who she is."

As if hearing our discussion, Stephanie slowly walked out of the house, tears streaming down her face. "Is she dead?"

"No," I growled. "She's going to be fine."

"I'm so s-sorry," Stephanie sobbed. "It's my fault. I just wanted... I don't know why, I can't explain why. I just... something has always been missing."

Cassius swore while Alex held up his hands and walked off in the other direction. "I'm taking the car. Let me know what you decide. I can't watch this."

Stephanie wiped her cheeks. "I'll help you take her to the room. Maybe if she's in some place familiar, she'll wake up."

I grunted and pushed past Stephanie. "Maybe."

"Ethan..." Stephanie croaked. "You have to believe me. I'm so sorry."

"I know," I whispered hoarsely. "I know." With a curse, I turned to Cassius. "Tell her, or I will."

Stephanie sniffed. "Tell me what?"

Cassius seemed to pale in that instant, all at once, as he swayed on his feet, gripping the door with both hands. "Stephanie..."

"What?" She looked between us. "Cassius, what's wrong with you? Why do you look so weak?"

"He saved Genesis," I answered.

Realization dawned on Stephanie's face as she stumbled back from both of us. "When she wakes up... she'll belong to him."

I didn't say anything because I didn't know what would happen, and neither did Cassius.

"Possibly," Cassius finally said.

Stephanie choked out a sob and ran past both of us and up the stairs.

"Cassius," I growled. "Tell her."

"Yeah." He licked his lips. "Just let me catch my breath first."

"It won't get easier with time."

"I know." He hung his head. "Let me just... give me just..." He shook his head. "Something's wrong."

"Cassius?"

"Very wrong." His eyes narrowed until they were fully white then black, tiny pinpricks. "I think I'm dying."

The last sentence he uttered before falling to the ground.

CHAPTER FORTY-TWO

Genesis

SARIEL WAS STANDING WITH ME, HOLDING my hand. It felt good. He wasn't so cold anymore, mostly warm like me.

"His blood calls to you," Sariel whispered.

"Who?" I felt happy, complete, yet a part of me missed something, like I was staring at a really pretty picture, but it was missing something epic, something that would change my world.

"Cassius and Ethan, both of their blood fights for you right now. I'm afraid you must yet again make a choice."

I sighed, my heart remembering Ethan, my mate, my love. "He's so warm. Why is Cassius cold?"

"Opposites, I suppose." Sariel squeezed my hand. "It was never meant to be like this, Genesis."

"Like what?" I continued watching the waves crash in front of me. He'd brought me to the beach. It was calming, beautiful.

"This..." Sariel held out his hand. "Dark Ones were never meant to exist, but it seems a human is just like a siren in the sense that their blood sings to angels in a way immortals' does not."

"Was Cassius's mom beautiful like him?"

"Yes." Sariel hung his head. "And she died just like Ara."

"Because she loved you?"

Sariel was quiet then whispered, "Because I loved her — too much."

"How can you love someone too much?"

"When that love overcomes all sense of reality and logic — when the love once beautiful starts to create fear and jealousy. Just because something starts out good does not mean it ends good. Do you understand?"

I sighed and laid my head on his shoulder. "You aren't good, but you aren't bad either. You're simply both."

"That I am." Sariel sighed. "His blood still calls. When you return to them, you'll have to make a choice, Genesis, but it's yours. Not theirs. Cassius gave you his essence."

"Will he die because of it?"

Sariel closed his eyes; a blue tear slid down his cheek, hitting me in the shoulder. "That depends on the balance of things."

"But..." I frowned. "I thought balance was restored."

"Yours... Ethan's." Sariel rubbed my hand. "But Cassius is still very much unbalanced. That's what love does to a Dark One. It is also why it is forbidden."

My eyes welled with tears. "He loves Stephanie... in that way?"

"He stayed away from the girl for a very long time... pushed her so far out of his mind, out of his consciousness, that he simply rejected the idea of even knowing her. When a female was needed, as an Elder I put the suggestion in his mind, made him think it was his own... made him think he was powerful enough to face his past in hopes he could finally start living."

"Instead, he got worse." I sighed.

"Because every day her smile reminds him of what he can

never have."

"There's always a way," I argued.

Sariel let out a laugh. "And this is why I like humans, always optimistic."

"What other choice do we have?"

His eyes met mine. "Exactly."

CHAPTER FORTY-THREE

Ethan

NOT HOW I EXPECTED TO START my day or end it.

Cassius was in the room next door to mine.

Genesis still hadn't woken up, but her breathing had evened out. Her heartbeat sounded less erratic. I had faith she was just healing — taking her time.

"Have you tried kissing her?" Mason said from the doorway.

"What?"

"Kissing her." Mason walked into the room, his arms folded, eyes tense. "In those movies, the prince always kisses the princess."

"What the hell are you talking about?" I growled. "What movies?"

"Like the King Lion movie... there's tons of them. I had nothing else to do, so I went out and bought them because they made Genesis happy, and I was losing my mind with worry so I watched a few... or maybe... seven... and the prince always kisses the princess."

I fought hard for patience as my fangs elongated, wanting

to take a bite out of his silly neck. "You watched cartoons. All day?"

"I made steak..." Mason fidgeted with his hands. "...for when she'd return. I thought maybe we could share it."

I glanced back at Genesis. "She would like that."

"I figured it would give her something to look forward to."

"Sharing meat with a wolf?" I smirked.

"And watching cartoons." Mason pulled a seat up to the bed. "And it's worth a shot. Maybe kiss her, then tell her about the steak."

Werewolves.

"Any change with Cassius?"

Mason shook his head. "His temperature drops for seconds before it skyrockets again. It's like he doesn't have enough blood to self-heal."

"He gave it all to her." Tears filled my eyes. "To save my mate."

"There must be something we can do for him," Mason growled. "He's still king. He's still..."

"Our friend. Brother," I finished. "Watch her for me? I need to find Stephanie."

Mason's face was impassive, but I could hear his heart pick up speed. "So, you'll risk breaking her heart by telling her the truth?"

"Yes." I licked my lips.

"Good luck." Mason shook his head. "I think I'll stay here and talk to Genesis about steak."

I smiled — the first time in a few hours — and patted him on the back. "Don't leave out any juicy details, wolf."

"Wouldn't dream of it," he growled then leaned over the bed and grabbed Genesis's hand. "Listen, human, if you don't wake up soon, I'm going to eat all the meat, and we both know what that would do to my digestive system at this point."

I let out a chuckle and moved down the hallway, my ears

sensitive to all the heartbeats in the house.

Cassius was weak, so weak. I'd never heard his heart flutter that way.

Another strong heartbeat joined the mix.

Picking up speed.

I waited as Stephanie reached the top of the stairs. Her hair was piled in a knot on her head, her blue eyes still blurred with tears.

"Remove it," I whispered.

Alex could hear my thoughts — could hear me in the house. He'd just walked in the door when I'd uttered the command. He cursed a blue streak.

"I said..." My voice edged with venom. "Remove it."

Alex's tortured heart slowed, and then the house trembled as Stephanie's hair went from light to dark, her lips from cherry to pale, her eyes — white.

She stumbled back and felt her face.

It would feel different, smoother, stronger.

Her hands shook in front of her. "What did you just do?"

"We need to talk." I held out my hand. "Trust me?"

She gulped, her white eyes blinking in confusion. "I feel different."

"Because you are."

"I don't understand."

"But you want to?"

She nodded.

"Take my hand."

The minute her fingers touched mine, she gasped. We'd always felt warm to one another, but the minute her skin came into contact with mine, frost formed across her fingertips.

"But—"

"Let's go visit Cassius. He may be sleeping right now, but I believe he'd want to be in the room."

"He hates me."

"No." I sighed. "That's where you're wrong."

"Dark Ones do not love," she whispered. "I know that now."

I tilted my head and smiled sadly. "Don't they?"

CHAPTER FORTY-FOUR

Genesis

"IT'S TIME." SARIEL RELEASED MY HAND.

"Will I see you again?"

He laughed, his feathers ruffling next to me. "Do you really want to?"

I shrugged. "You're not so bad."

"So many compliments my head may explode."

He wasn't. It was weird. He was dangerous; he had potential for both evil and good, but he was also in a position where he had no choice but to force the rules on people — and hope that in the end everything worked out. I felt sorry for him.

Sariel tilted my chin toward him. "Don't."

Tears filled my eyes. "Thank you... for staying with me."

"Always." He plucked a purple feather from his wings and placed it in my hands. "I'm only a thought away."

I clenched the feather in my hands and nodded. "Goodbye."

His lips touched my forehead as cold spilled through my body, followed by such intense heat that I started to convulse.

I saw Ethan's warm smile... the first time he'd bitten me, our shared kisses, our mouths fusing together as if we needed each other so desperately we would die without touch.

And then Cassius — his heart of ice — shattering, breaking, and transforming into something beautiful right before my very eyes as his lips met mine, and he whispered, "Breathe."

I wanted to breathe.

But not him, not Cassius.

I tried to yell for Ethan.

Clenching the feather tighter in my hands, I fought. Fought for the warmth like it was the only way I would see him again. The cold threatened; it also offered me peace.

While the heat reminded me of the mating, of the severe pain I'd had to go through in order to be his—

I would go through it all over again.

Through the fires of hell to be with Ethan.

I embraced the heat, holding out my hands as the fires singed my fingertips. I welcomed the pain — because would it really be worth it if it was easy? If loving him was that simple?

Fire exploded in my chest, pinching, trickling down my fingertips until my knees buckled beneath me.

There was no relief.

And I was okay with it — I welcomed it. Because soon — I would be with Ethan again.

"Steak," something whispered.

I cried out. Had I heard that right? Steak?

"Lots of steak and other meat. Hell, I'll get you your own butcher... I think Belle had a butcher? Or maybe that was another princess."

What?

The fire got hotter and hotter.

"I told him it was true love's kiss, but does he listen? No, just walks off and lets me talk about food. I have a confession. I hate berries."

Mason? I tried to speak his name, but my mouth was too hot; when I opened it, more heat entered, stealing my breath.

"And pinecones taste like shit, but hey, a wolf does what a wolf does. It's not like it will kill me. Do you think I'm grumpy like the beast?"

I smiled, focusing on Mason's voice as the pain increased. *Keep talking!* I wanted to yell. *Just keep saying something!*

"Don't expect me to sing — wolves do not sing."

I smiled.

"Aw, was that a twitch of your lips, human? Alright, I'll tell you something else... something you can never speak of again. When I was a pup, I had a pet caterpillar... cried when the damn thing turned into a butterfly. Circle of life... hey, that's King Lion's song!"

A laugh escaped between my lips as I tried to open my eyes. They felt like sandpaper.

"Come on," Mason urged. "You know you want the steak."

I shook my head back and forth, and then finally, with great effort, opened my eyes.

Mason grinned. "Green. Your eyes are very, very green."

CHAPTER FORTY-FIVE

Ethan

I GRABBED STEPHANIE BY THE ARM and gently led her into the room where Cassius was sleeping — resting — hopefully healing.

The minute we stepped inside the door, I could see my breath leave my lips. Frost lined his body; his lips were completely blue.

He shuddered in his sleep, reaching his hand up to the ceiling only to drop it down again by his side.

"What's wrong with him?" A tear froze on Stephanie's pale cheek.

I sighed, running my hand through my hair. "I have no idea."

"You mean, he's never been like this before? In all the years you've known him?" Her eyes were accusing. Then again, she was scared for him — she loved him.

"Just how old do you think I am?" I fired back. "And no." I released her hand. "I've never seen him like this. I can hear his heart... it's slow."

She slowly made her way to his side and reached for his

hand. The minute she touched him, the temperature in the room rose a few degrees, I could taste it on my tongue, taste the heat of life building, boiling inside him.

"I can't explain it." Her eyes locked on him. I imagined she couldn't look away even if she wanted to. "The pull he has on me. Like I've known him my whole life — like I've waited for him—" She hung her head. "Or maybe like he's been waiting for me. It's stupid." Her laugh was hollow. "I know it's stupid, but I can't help it."

"Stephanie..." I took a seat across from her. "It's not stupid... because a very long time ago... there was an innocent little girl caught in the middle of a war that should have never been started. He saved her life and, in return, hid her true identity from herself."

"What?"

The easiest way was to show her, so I bit into my wrist and held the blood to her lips. "Drink and see."

"I've never drunk vampire blood."

"Yes, well, this is a day of firsts." I rolled my eyes. "Just know it's going to burn going down, always does for your kind."

"Sirens?"

My throat was thick with emotion. "No. Dark Ones."

Her mouth dropped open. I took advantage and shoved what I could of my wrist past her lips. The minute the blood entered her body, her head fell back, eyes white, mouth open.

I closed my own eyes and focused in on the exact memory I needed to pull.

Cassius in the Orchard with Stephanie.

Stephanie and Alex.

Him wiping her memories.

And finally, her waving goodbye.

It broke my heart all over again to feel his sadness — to experience his loss as if it was my own.

With a gasp, Stephanie opened her eyes and stared at

Cassius. "He saved my life."

"He did."

"He..." Tears streamed down her cheeks. "He promised I would never forget him." Her lips trembled. "He lied."

"He had to protect you — at all costs. Dark Ones are no longer made, Stephanie. You know that. He's one of the oldest, one of ten who were allowed to live."

"But I'm alive," she whispered, touching her fingertips to her mouth. "I should be dead."

"Yes, well... Genesis made an offer Sariel couldn't refuse."

Stephanie covered her face with her hands. "Tell me she didn't sacrifice herself for everyone."

I didn't deny it. "And when she did Cassius offered her immortality — something that only he was strong enough to give — to bring her back from the brink of death."

"And now he's cold... dying."

"We don't know that," I said in a soft voice. "But I do know he needs you... he needs your blood."

Stephanie's gaze snapped to mine. "Would it work?"

"No idea." I licked my lips and stood. "But it's worth a try." I cringed at the thought of Mason's advice but offered it nonetheless. "The werewolf seems to think a kiss does the trick."

Stephanie's lips twitched. "He never let me kiss him."

"But I thought you spent the evenings with him and —"

"Talked." A rosy hue pinched her cheeks. "I just wanted to be by him. For some reason, his touch never affected me the same way it did others. It was comforting, familiar, so I've been pestering him every night for the past few years. At first he only let me visit once a year, after I'd come of age... and then it quickly turned into once a month, once a week, every night."

"He cares for you," I said. "I'm sure of it."

"I wish that was enough... caring." She gripped his hand tighter. "But maybe I can love him enough for both of us."

"Nobody deserves to live that way, Stephanie, regardless of what he did."

"He saved my life," she said simply. "How selfish of a person would I have to be to not offer him the same kindness, regardless of how I feel for him?"

"Dark Ones have never tried to bond to one another — ever."

"I know."

"You could die."

"I know."

"I didn't bring you in here to save him... but to give you the truth."

"Then thank you," Stephanie stood and kissed me on the cheek, "for giving me both."

In an instant she turned in my arms and lunged for Cassius. The room plummeted in a blanket of cold as she leaned over him.

"I'll need your teeth, Ethan." She held her arm behind her.

I bit deep.

Pain marred her features, and then she was in my arms. "On the lips."

"What?"

Before I could react, she turned her mouth against my fangs, slicing open her bottom lip.

The tinge of angel blood hit my tongue just as she once again leaned over Cassius and kissed his mouth, breathing out the word, "Live."

CHAPTER FORTY-SIX

Genesis

"GREEN?" I REPEATED. "LIKE ETHAN-GREEN or milky green?"

"What the hell does milky green mean?" Mason scowled. "And they're Ethan-green — almost creepy."

My face cracked into a wide smile. "Does that mean I'm a vampire now?"

"Does your face itch?"

"What?"

Mason shrugged. "Does it itch?"

"No."

"Do you smell berries?"

"Huh?"

"Just answer the question," he growled.

I sniffed the air. "No, I smell... wood burning."

He grinned. "Then you aren't a werewolf."

"Gee, thanks." I tried to get up, but he moved around me and tugged my body to a sitting position. "I was worried there for a second. Do werewolves really smell berries?"

"Sometimes." He chuckled, brushing a kiss across my forehead. "To vampires we smell like burning wood...

outdoors, warm."

I nodded and leaned in. "I like the way you smell."

"Care to keep your paws to yourself, Mason?" Ethan said from the door, his grimace turning into a grin as he strode in and practically threw Mason off me and pulled me into his arms. "Your eyes are green."

"Why do people keep telling me what color my eyes are?"

"Because," Mason said from his spot behind Ethan, "it's a sign."

"Of what?"

"Greatness." Ethan's mouth found mine; his tongue tasted like sugar.

With a moan, I threw my arms around his neck and tugged him harder against me.

Mason coughed.

Ethan waved him away, moving onto the bed, pulling my body tightly against his.

Our mouths were fused together. I never wanted to let go — never wanted to breathe if it wasn't heavy with his taste, his scent.

I forgot about the feather in my hands, pushing it against his chest.

Ethan flinched and pulled back with a hiss. "Sariel?"

I nodded. "He was with me... when I closed my eyes."

"Well, I'll be damned," Mason muttered under his breath. "The archangels rarely visit immortals, and now you're saying you spent actual time with him?"

"After my kidnapping," I muttered.

"Doesn't matter." Mason's eyebrows shot up. "Time is their currency, to spend time with any being — when you're an angel — is a gift."

I lifted the feather to my face, the purple shining in the light of the room.

Ethan reached out and touched the edges of the feather. "When an angel gives one of his feathers, it's like wishing on a star. Tell me, what did Sariel say to you?"

"He said to choose," I whispered, and he gave me the feather.

"The desire of your heart." Ethan's eyes shone with green. "Cassius may have saved you — granted you immortality — but it was Sariel who let you choose how you'd return."

"I just..." I gripped Ethan by the shoulders. "I just wanted you."

"You have me," he vowed, kissing my mouth hard, "for an eternity."

Mason coughed again.

"Then leave!" Ethan growled over his shoulder. "Nobody's asking you to watch."

A loud male scream pierced the air.

"Cassius," Mason and Ethan said in unison.

In a flash, I was in Ethan's arms, being carried into the room next to us. He set me on my feet just as Cassius jerked up from the bed, his eyes white, veins in his neck pulsing blue.

Stephanie braced herself over him protectively.

He reached for her arms, gripping her shoulders so hard I wanted to flinch on her behalf. "What have you done?"

"What needed to be done," she whispered.

With a groan, he touched his forehead to hers gently, something that seemed odd for him to do. He was always so abrasive, big, looming, scary.

It was then I noticed that Stephanie didn't look the same. Her hair was black, her eyes matching Cassius's.

Alex entered the room.

The temperature rose a few degrees. I felt like a fight was about to break out. But instead of Alex lunging for anyone, he simply gripped the wall and watched as if fascinated by what was taking place.

"What did she do?" I whispered in Ethan's ear.

Ethan's eyes narrowed, searching.

I followed his gaze and nearly fell to my knees when I saw

the blood drenching Stephanie's chest.

"She gave him... her heart." Ethan's hoarse voice pierced the silence in the room. "The only good a Dark One possesses."

"Wait? What does that mean?" I asked.

Right before my eyes, Stephanie's glow faded. Her eyes turned blue, her hair stayed black, but her skin was no longer glowing.

"It means," Cassius's voice rumbled, "she gave her essence, her immortality, to me."

Alex sighed from the door. "It means she's now human."

Stephanie nodded slowly and whispered, "It was worth it."

CHAPTER FORTY-SEVEN

Ethan

I'D NEVER SEEN IT ACTUALLY DONE before — an immortal giving essence to another. Only Dark Ones were fully capable of doing it. They were the strongest, after all.

And now. She was nothing.

Stephanie swayed toward Cassius.

He caught her body with his hands, his eyes swirling white. "Why would you do this?"

Stephanie squinted as if she was having trouble focusing. "Because a long time ago, you saved a little girl who should have died. It was the least I could do."

I watched the scene unfold. Something was off. Stephanie wasn't dying, not that I thought she would, but Cassius was—

"Cassius!" I yelled. "Stop touching her!"

Cassius frowned and looked down at his hands. They were still touching her skin, but Stephanie wasn't acting like a typical human being touched by a Dark One. Usually they were filled with so much lust that they attacked, and their arousal was so evident you could smell it in the air.

I smelled absolutely nothing but my own mate and every

other person in that room.

No lust.

"Well..." Alex chuckled from the door. "How's that for a fun twist to the story? The great Dark One has no effect on Stephanie as a human."

I was relieved.

Cassius looked irritated.

He moved his hands down her arms then back up again, his face twisting with curiosity until he finally cupped her chin. "You feel nothing?"

Stephanie shrugged. "You feel a bit cold, but other than that, it's nice to be touched."

"Nice..." Cassius repeated. "Nice?"

"Bad answer," Genesis said under her breath.

I wrapped my arm tighter around her, tugging the warmth of her body against mine.

Cassius continued inspecting Stephanie as if he couldn't understand why she wasn't affected by him.

"You would know if she was lying," I finally pointed out. "And Stephanie, you should rest."

She nodded, suppressing a yawn with her hand. When she rose, she leaned over and kissed Cassius on the cheek. "I'm glad you're okay."

Cassius's face was priceless.

Never in his existence had he ever had any creature not be affected by his presence. I imagined it was a humbling experience — one he didn't enjoy.

"Thank you." He released her, his arms falling to his sides as if they carried the weight of the world.

She stumbled toward us.

Alex moved quickly, lifting her into his arms. "You know, you're still my sister... in every way that matters."

"Ha." She yawned. "So you won't disown me?"

"Not unless you really piss me off — then again, you are a human. By the way, do I affect you? Feeling warm and tingly?"

She frowned. "First of all, gross... second, no."

"Fascinating." Mason rubbed his chin and shook his head. "It must be because she started out immortal."

Cassius was still staring at the door long after Alex had carried her out of it.

"I need to talk to him," I whispered into Genesis's hair.

She nodded and held out her hand to Mason. "I believe you promised we'd share a steak?"

"You heard that?" Mason growled.

"All of it." She grinned. "Come on, feed me, wolf."

He smiled and tucked her into his body. "I'll feed you, but I may need help with my own eating habits."

"Together." She patted his chest. "Alright?"

He kissed her forehead and walked out with her.

Typically, I would have ripped his lips off for daring to graze her skin, but I felt her heart beat for me, saw her green eyes, knew without a shadow of a doubt that she loved me — and only me.

"Controlling your emotions well, I see," Cassius said in a low gravelly voice.

"One of us should," I fired back.

He looked away and cursed. "I have no idea what you're talking about."

"Oh?" I moved toward the bed and sat on the edge. "No idea at all?"

Cassius stared at the blankets.

I laughed. "Lie."

Mumbling another curse, he crossed his arms. "Dirty vampire trick, tasting the air to see if I'm being honest."

"Well..." I shrugged. "At least be honest with yourself. You're disappointed."

"It's called shock. Hasn't happened in a great while... I imagine it will pass." He licked his lips only to have those same lips covered in frost again.

"You love her."

"Dark Ones don't love."

"I really wish people would stop saying that when all evidence points to the contrary." I arched my eyebrows. "She's human now."

"Thanks, caught that."

"You could mate with her."

Cassius went very still.

I kept talking. "She's immune. She wouldn't become addicted or obsessed."

"Right," he croaked.

"Fear..." I tilted my head. "Now I taste fear. Odd, since Dark Ones are afraid of nothing."

"It's a day of firsts. I should sleep."

"You rarely sleep."

Cassius pounded the mattress with his fist. "Damn it! Why didn't she just let me pass? Things would have been so much easier."

"Do you truly want easy?"

"No."

"Cassius—"

"No!" He pointed at the door. "That woman... that, that—" He bit down into his lip. "She'll ruin me."

"How do you figure?"

"Because I'll fail."

"I think you lost me."

Cassius pushed the dark hair from his face and swallowed. "I don't know the first thing about honestly pursuing someone or something without using every ounce of power I possess. To Stephanie, I may as well be human."

"And that's so bad?"

"It's horrible." His eyes met mine. "Because I'll be found wanting."

"So insecure."

"Honest," he said in a humorless laugh. "She couldn't

possibly want me, darkness and all, and even if she did, I have no power to convince her of anything."

"So don't use your power."

His nostrils flared.

"Don't pursue her as a Dark One..." I whispered. "Pursue her as a man."

Cassius closed his eyes and leaned back against the headboard. "Or I simply don't do anything."

I burst out laughing at the way his heart picked up pace. "I'd really like to see you try."

"You don't think I'm strong enough?" he roared.

"No." I shrugged and got up. "I think you're tired of fighting what's been in front of you too damn long, but good luck with your plan. I'm sure that will work out really well, you miserable bastard."

"Since when do you talk to your king like this?"

"Since I realized he's more friend, more brother, than king."

Cassius's lips twitched. "Don't let that get around. Imagine what it would do to my horrible reputation."

Laughing, I turned on my heel and walked toward the door. "Cassius?"

"Hmm?" He lifted his head.

"You owe it to you, and you owe it to her to at least try."

"And fail?"

"Trying isn't near as fun when you already know you'll succeed."

"Go find your mate. I'm tired of you making sense, vampire."

Smirking, I waved him off and made my way downstairs, passing Stephanie's room on the way. Alex was just leaving, his expression amused.

"What?" My eyes narrowed.

"She's human."

"So?"

"I just find it funny." Alex slapped me on the back. "We gain a human a few days ago only to lose her and gain another."

I stopped walking. "Genesis is still human."

Alex tilted his head. "Her heart still beats, yes. But..." His smile grew. "Interesting. You didn't even notice."

"Notice?" I gripped him by the shirt and slammed him against the wall. "Notice what?"

"Holy shit!" Mason screamed from the kitchen.

Alex burst out laughing. "I think you're about to find out, poor Mason. I do hope he was able to get away in time."

CHAPTER FORTY-EIGHT

Genesis

"MASON!" I COVERED MY MOUTH WITH my hands — my very sharp mouth. "I'm so sorry! I don't know what came over me!"

His mouth was still open, maybe in shock, possibly a bit of horror as he looked from the raw steak back to me. "Blood."

I shook my head. "It just — I didn't—"

Mason roared with laughter then carefully set the knife down and made his way around the table. "Fangs look good on you."

I covered my mouth again. "But I'm human."

"Vampires get very protective when they feel threatened." He held up his hands then tilted his head. "May I?"

"What?"

He winked and leaned down, pressing his head against my stomach. Was he insane?

"Mason, please, tell me why the hell you have your head pressed against my mate before I rip your tongue out."

"Such violence," Alex said in an amused voice. "You'll have to learn to guard what you say when you have a little person running around."

"Little person?" Ethan repeated.

"Shh…" Alex held his finger to his lips. "…listen."

Ethan stared at me then at Mason then at Alex. "Three heartbeats, but—"

"But…" Alex nodded. "Do you hear that fourth one? Kind of sounds like a horse taking off, its hooves hitting the race track in rapid succession."

Mason grinned and looked up at me. "Healthy."

"Wh-what?" I was still covering my mouth.

"Vampire blood…" Mason laughed and slapped his knee as he sat down. "For one reason or another the mixture of the bloody steak and me holding a knife set your heart racing. Protective vampire blood took over, compliments of your mate and newfound immortality, and here we are…"

"I attacked you!" I wanted to crawl under the table and hide.

"To protect your little one." Mason winked. "It won't be the last time."

"Little one," Ethan repeated still as a statue.

Alex grinned between all of us. "I'd like to point out I knew first."

"How?" Ethan growled.

"I counted." Alex rolled his eyes. "The heartbeat was so faint at first. I thought it was because we were losing Cassius, and then when Genesis walked in, it was stronger. And we all know what happens when a mate is made immortal. They take on different… gifts… from their immortal partner. She's still human, but mama bear will most definitely fang a bitch or…" He smirked. "…a werewolf — my apologies — if she feels threatened."

Mason let out a low growl while Ethan moved around the table and gathered me into his arms. "You're pregnant."

"Um…" I gulped. "Apparently."

"Immortals move fast and all that." Alex yawned. "Oh,

and here's some good news. Six months — not nine. Immortal blood develops faster."

I nodded my head, unsure if what I was hearing was actually happening. "I think... I think I need to sit."

"Yes, well, just keep your fangs in." Ethan grinned.

Horrified, I touched my mouth again only to find the fangs gone. "What happened?"

"Retracted." Alex winked. "Cool trick, right?"

"Alex, don't you have somewhere to be?" Ethan hissed.

"No." Alex pulled out a chair. "I really don't, and it's *Uncle* Alex."

Mason grinned.

"Does that make me a grandfather?" Cassius stumbled into the room. "Because as much as a new life excites me, I'm the oldest here, and the thought doesn't sit well with me." He winced and pulled out a seat.

"Hip bothering you again?" Alex joked.

Cassius tilted his head, white filling his eyes, while Alex jumped out of his chair and started scratching his arms violently. "Make it stop."

Cassius smirked. "I have no idea what you're talking about, siren."

Ethan rolled his eyes. "Cassius..."

"Fine," Cassius snapped, his eyes flashed, and Alex stopped itching.

"You know I hate ants," Alex grumbled, crossing his arms. "Making me see one of my fears isn't a good way to make friends."

"I have friends." Cassius shrugged.

I smiled and reached for him. Ethan's eyes were leery, but I knew it would be okay, knew that touching Cassius would do nothing to me.

He must have realized it too because the minute my hand snaked out, Cassius clenched it with his and kissed me on the knuckles. "I'm glad you're feeling better."

"Me too." I squeezed his hand back and then kissed his cheek.

Ethan growled.

"Settle." Cassius rolled his eyes. "She feels nothing for me. Her heart is pure green."

"Funny," Ethan hissed.

"Like her eyes." Cassius smiled.

"I only have four steaks." Mason interjected. "So, if you guys need more food, someone has to go to the store, and I vote Alex, since he's the most irritating of the group."

"I don't eat." Cassius frowned. "But..."

I laughed and pointed to the meat. "Maybe you should try to be more human."

"She has a point." Ethan pulled me into his lap. "It may help things along."

"Things?" Alex squinted. "What things?"

Cassius growled.

Alex's eyes narrowed. "Oh no. Hell, no."

Mason chuckled. "So, we get more steak."

"Am I the only one who thinks this is a really bad idea?" Alex shouted.

"What idea?" I played dumb, knowing exactly what was going to happen. Cassius was going to pursue Stephanie... as he should.

"I'll murder you," Alex said in a low voice.

"Any more fears, Alex?" Cassius taunted.

"Bastard."

"King." His eyes flashed. "And don't you forget it."

CHAPTER FORTY-NINE

Ethan

THE MINUTE I'D DISCOVERED SHE WAS pregnant, it was like I'd ceased to exist, and every thought focused on the tiny life growing inside of her.

I couldn't stop staring at her all throughout dinner. I didn't want to eat food. I wanted to taste her — taste and make sure the baby was healthy — and force my own blood down her throat even if I had to trick her. It would make the baby grow faster.

And I'd feel a hell of a lot better about protecting both their lives.

"Stop fidgeting," Alex said to my left. "You're worse than a woman."

"Don't call me a woman," I snarled, trying to pay attention to the card game, while Genesis and Mason attempted to bake a cake.

She wanted chocolate.

He had some extra berries for the toppings.

And now they deemed themselves professionals. Pans went flying, and I knew it was only a matter of time before my gourmet kitchen was going to have dings all over it from both Mason's inability to do anything gentle and Genesis's newfound strength.

A knife had impaled itself into Alex's thigh when she was cutting vegetables. Don't ask me how. One minute it had been in her hand; the next minute it had gone flying. Naturally, I'd gotten out of the way.

Alex, however, had been too busy daydreaming.

He'd bled for mere seconds before he healed.

But he was still irritated.

It was torture — waiting for the cake to bake. Waiting for everyone to stop talking.

Waiting, waiting, waiting.

Finally, Cassius cleared his throat and whispered something in Genesis's ear before giving me a fleeting look and walking out of the room.

She jumped to her feet, reached for my hand, and the next thing I knew, she was pulling me up the stairs toward our bedroom.

The doors slammed behind us.

And her mouth was on mine.

"You taste like chocolate," I growled, biting at her lips. "Sweet."

"Mmm..." She gripped my hair with her hands, jumped into my arms, and wrapped her legs around me. "...and you taste like sugar."

I chuckled and bit at her lips again. Tasting a bit of her blood mixed with her scent had my mind racing as I tossed her onto the bed and ripped at her clothes aggressively. "I've been wanting to do this for hours."

"Rip clothes?" she teased.

"Only yours."

"I didn't know." Genesis tilted her head back while my lips found her neck, trailing kisses all the way down until I came into contact with her bra — worthless piece of material. I ripped it off and made a mental note not to let her wear any undergarments — ever. Too many unnecessary layers.

She let out a moan when I licked between the valley of her breasts, my mouth making a wet trail down her stomach.

"Cassius said we needed alone time."

"Remind me to vote him into office." I swirled my tongue around her belly button and moved lower, tugging her leggings away. Damn, she wore a lot of clothes. Where the hell were all those dresses I told Stephanie to buy for her?

"You vote for king?"

"Stop talking," I hissed, licking her hipbone then biting the sensitive flesh above it.

"O-o-okay." Genesis gripped my head and forced it down.

I chuckled. "Demanding."

"Sorry, I was... distracted."

"Allow me to distract you more." I leaned up on my knees, still hovering over her and ripped off every stitch of clothing left on my body. "Also, remind me to lock you in the bedroom for the next few weeks."

She laughed, her hands dancing across my naked chest. "You're beautiful."

"Vampires are deadly. Not beautiful."

"Fine. You're deadly."

I smiled.

"Still pretty though."

"Dangerous," I corrected her.

Her eyebrows arched.

With a hiss, I flipped her onto her stomach and moved between her thighs. "Still think I'm pretty?"

"Very." She moved up to her knees and looked over her shoulder. "Is this you trying to prove me wrong?"

With a growl, I rocked her hips back, plunging into her. "Guess I'll have to try harder."

"Yes, harder." She closed her eyes and whimpered.

With a growl, I filled her and began slowly stroking,

moving. I ducked my head down and bit the side of her hip, drawing blood between my lips as I went deeper, filling every inch of her.

Eternity.

Immortality.

I experienced it only with Genesis.

And I knew my life would never be the same. Because she lived... I was forever changed.

"Ethan!" she screamed.

I pulled out and flipped her onto her back, sinking my fangs into her neck as I thrust one last time, nearly taking us both off the bed. "I love you," I whispered hoarsely against her neck. "Forever."

EPILOGUE

Cassius

I WANDERED THE STREETS, LETTING THE darkness consume the loneliness inside my chest. The irritating little jab that continued to beat in a melodic rhythm, reminding me that I was alive.

That she'd almost died.

I muttered a curse and pulled the hood of my jacket over my head, moving through the shadows, watching, waiting.

"You called?" an amused voice cracked into the night sky.

I flinched at the way his every syllable made my body want to convulse with anger — rage. "Yes."

"And?"

"She gave me her immortality. Is it possible to give it back?"

He stepped out of the shadows, his white hair a stark contrast to the dark air swirling around us, protecting us from watchful eyes. "Why would you want to do that?"

I hated my father, hated Sariel for forcing me into the position of king over a people who, for the most part, feared me but despised me with a hateful rage that could never be fixed. "She's weak."

Sariel smiled, folding his large arms across his chest in a manner that reminded me what he was — and what I was in comparison. Small. "There is always a way to return what has been given, but things always come at a cost. You give back the gift — you earn the same fate."

I figured as much.

"Being human, is it so horrible?" Sariel held his hands out in front of him as the cloud of darkness disappeared and people walked around us, mindless of our presence. "Some of them are happy."

"But most of them are full of fear, anger, sadness." I shook my head. "The same emotions that would overtake me if I didn't have your blood."

Sariel's eyes flashed white. "Emotions are something we don't readily experience."

I licked my lips and nodded once. "Thank you."

His eyebrows shot up. "That's a first."

I ignored him and turned my back, walking in the other direction. It was a mistake to call for him, a mistake to meet with him — only to find out that I was in the same damn position I'd been in a few days ago.

In love.

Chasing after something so forbidden that I'd risked my life in order to follow my heart.

"Thirty days," Sariel called behind me.

I glanced over my shoulder. "Thirty days?"

"Thirty days of humanity — learn to love as a human does. If she loves you in return, truly loves you as you are and mates with you, I'll restore your immortality — and allow her hers."

My heart picked up speed in my chest. "And if I fail?"

Sarial grinned menacingly. "Then I kill you. Blood must always be shed for balance. You know that by now, son."

"Thirty days," I repeated.

"Thirty days, oh, and do try not to get shot or develop a sickness that's not yet found a cure."

"I haven't agreed."

"You agreed the minute the words fell upon your ears." Sariel raised his hands above his head.

A clap of thunder sounded.

Severe pain ripped through my legs as I fell to my knees onto the cold wet pavement.

Heart racing, I reached for my chest only to find that my skin was warm to the touch.

"Thirty days," he whispered and disappeared.

Shaking, I rose to my feet, stumbling past buildings. When I finally made it out of the alleyway and into the light up street, I glanced at my reflection in the store window and almost got sick.

My skin had color.

And my eyes... were blue.

ABOUT THE AUTHOR

RACHEL VAN DYKEN is the *New York Times, Wall Street Journal,* and *USA Today* bestselling author of regency and contemporary romances. When she's not writing you can find her drinking coffee at Starbucks and plotting her next book while watching "The Bachelor".

She keeps her home in Idaho with her husband, adorable son, and two snoring boxers. She loves to hear from readers.

You can connect with her on Facebook at facebook.com/rachelvandyken or join her fan group *Rachel's New Rockin Readers*. Her website is www.rachelvandykenauthor.com.

ACKNOWLEDGEMENTS

I'M SO THANKFUL to the amazing editors who worked on this book with me! Laura Heritage, Paula Buckendorf, and Katherine Tate! You guys are AMAZING and always do such an incredible job!

To my publicist Danielle Sanchez and the rest of the crew at Inkslinger, thank you for always having my back and making sure each release is incredible!

The Rockin' Readers fan group, wow, you guys seriously stepped it up and helped me with this book and didn't laugh when I said, hey I think I'm going to write a vampire novel. Thank you for hanging out with me on a daily basis and helping me with these fun projects!

ALL THE BLOGGERS, ah, you guys, seriously. I can't even express my gratitude for all that you do.

Erica, you're the best agent a girl could ask for!

Nate, thanks for not getting irritated when dinner burns because I'm busy finishing just one more chapter.

And last but not least, I thank God every day that I'm able to do what I love! He's everything.

www.rachelvandykenauthor.com

13735586R00158

Printed in Great Britain
by Amazon.co.uk, Ltd.,
Marston Gate.